A Tame Surrender,
A Story of The Chicago Strike

Charles King

Contents

A TAME SURRENDER,
A STORY OF THE CHICAGO STRIKE

BY

Charles King

A TAME SURRENDER.

CHAPTER I.

She had met him the previous summer on the Rhine, and now "if they aren't engaged they might as well be," said her friends, "for he is her shadow wherever she goes." There was something characteristically inaccurate about that statement, for Miss Allison was rather undersized in one way and oversized in another; at least that, too, is what her friends said. She was not more than five feet in height nor less than five feet in breadth "measured from tip to tip of her wings," as her brother said. Miss Allison had wings, not because she was an angel, but because it was the fashion,--wings that sprouted at her fair, plump, shapely shoulders and billowed out like balloons. Her brother Cary, above referred to, a sixteen-year-old specimen of Young American impudence and independence, said further of her, in the spring of '94, that if Floy's sleeves were only inflated with gas she could float on air as easily as she did on water, and on water Miss Allison was buoyancy personified. On water, too, and in her dainty bathing-dress, Miss Allison's wings were discarded and her true proportions more accurately defined. She was anything but slender. She was simply deliciously, exquisitely rounded *now*; but the question which so disturbed her feminine friends as to call for perennial repetition was, What *would* she be a few years hence? This, however, was a matter that seemed to give the lady in question no uneasiness whatever. Certainly it resulted in no loss of flesh. Perhaps it might have been better for her future figure if it had. With her perfect health, digestion, and disposition, there was absolutely no way of worrying off a pound or two a week. She was the soul of good nature and content. She had an indulgent father, a luxurious home, abundant wealth, an unimpeachable complexion, character, and social position. She had a swarm of enviously devoted girl friends on the one hand and selfishly devoted male admirers on the other, or on both if she chose. She was absolutely without a mean or unkind thought of anybody. She was full of every generous impulse. She was lazy and energetic by turns, had been a romping idler in her earlier school-days, and had been polished off and finished in an expensive Eastern establishment without finishing anything herself. She had lived an almost unshadowed life, had laughed off a dozen lovers when she went abroad in '93, and had then fallen in with her fate across the water.

There was really no excuse for her falling in love with Mr. Floyd Forrest. An utter dissimilarity to her other admirers, a romantic and somewhat absurd adventure, and, above all, proximity, were what did it. He must have been over ten years her senior; she was barely twenty when they met. He was tall, slender, and strong, with deep burning brown eyes and heavy brows and lashes. She was short and plump and distractingly fair and fresh and blue-eyed,--big melting blue eyes, too, they were. His lips were well-nigh hidden by a heavy moustache; hers were well-nigh faultless in their sweet, warm, rosy curves, faultless as the white, even teeth that gleamed in her merry laughter. He was reserved and taciturn, even gloomy at times, facts which, through no fault or connivance of hers, were presently explained and only served to heighten the interest she had begun to feel in him. She was frankness, almost loquacity itself,--a girl who could no more keep a secret than she could harbor a grudge. He was studious, thoughtful, forever reading. She loved air, sunshine, action, travel, tennis, dancing, music (of the waltz variety), and, beyond her Bible and her Baedeker, read nothing at all, and not too much of them! She was with her aunt and some American friends when first she met him. It was the morning they hove in sight of England, and the steamer was pitching through a head sea. Her party were wretchedly ill; she was aggressively well. She had risen early and gone up to the promenade deck in hopes of getting the first glimpse of Bishop's Rock, and found the spray dashing high over the bows, drenching her accustomed perch on the forward deck and keeping people within-doors.

It was too early for those who had been her beaux and gallants on the swift spring run; a late session in the smoking-room the night before had kept them below. Only one man was visible at the rail under the bridge,--the tall, dark, military-looking American who seemed to divide his time between reading and tramping on the promenade deck, pacing the planks with long, swinging stride and never seeming to care for other society than his own thoughts. He was on deck and keenly enjoying the strong, salt wind and its whistling load of spray; and, clinging to the stanchions at the saloon door, wistfully did Miss Allison regard him, but only as the means to an end. She wanted to get there, and did not see a way without a helping hand, and just here old Neptune seemed to tender it. A huge, foam-crested billow came sweeping straight from the invisible shores of Albion, burst in magnificent deluge upon the port bow, lifted high in air one instant the heaving black mass of the stem, then let it down with stomach-stirring swish deep into the hollow beyond,--deep, deep into the green mountain that followed, careening the laboring steamer far over to starboard, and shooting Miss Allison, as plump and pleasing a projectile as was ever catapulted, straight from the brass-bound door-way, across the slippery deck and into the stranger's welcoming arms. Springing suddenly back from under the bridge to avoid the coming torrent, Mr. Forrest was spun along the rail until nearly opposite the companion-way, and just in the nick of time.

"I think I'd have gone overboard if it hadn't been for you," said Miss Allison, all smiles and salt water, as she clung to the rail a moment later, while Mr. Forrest's steamer-cap, bumped off in the collision, rode helplessly astern on the crest of the hissing wave. "But I couldn't swim like your cap. Do take my Tam," she cried, tearing off her knitted head-gear and letting her soft, fair curls whip out into so many briny strings.

"I'll use this," he shouted, turning up the capote of his ulster, while the cape thrashed furiously in the wind. "Will you pardon my saying you are a trifle venturesome?"

"Oh, I love the ocean and the wind and the sea," she cried, enthusiastically. "Don't you pity people who are too ill or too lazy to get up and see this?" And she stretched forward one white, dimpled, dainty hand over the seething waters. "Dare we get over on the other side?"

"You couldn't stand there," he said, briefly, "and would be drenched if you could. Best stay here."

And stay they did until breakfast, by which time she had told him a great deal about herself and learned next to nothing about him.

"Remember," she said, "you are to give me your address, and I'm to send you a new steamer-cap to replace the one I knocked overboard." And he merely smiled, thanked her, said it was entirely unnecessary, but did not present the expected card at all. "Perhaps he hadn't any," suggested Aunt Lawrence, after they got into sheltered waters off the Start Point. "He doesn't look like a society man. There are so many of these commercial people travelling now."

"Oh, he didn't talk at all like a drummer," said Miss Allison in prompt defence of her new protector. "In fact, I don't think he talked at all."

"Not if you had first innings, Flo," drawled Master Cary, from the shelter of his steamer-rug. "He ain't a drummer, but like's not he's been one. He's an army officer. Hubbard said so." Hubbard was one of the belated admirers.

Whether soldier or not, however, Mr. Forrest did not prosecute the chance acquaintance. He lifted the successor to the shipwrecked cap on passing Miss Allison's party later in the day, but never approached them nearer, never seemed to see the invitation in Miss Allison's shining blue eyes. "Really, Cary," said she, as they neared Southampton, "you must go and get his address and the size of the steamer-cap." But Cary was the type of the traditional younger brother, a spoiled one at that, and Cary wouldn't. It was Mr. Hubbard who went on the mission and came back with the man.

"Pray don't think of getting me a cap," said Mr. Forrest, bowing and smiling rather gravely. "I'd much rather you did not. Indeed, it wouldn't find me, as I make no stay in England at all. I--I wish you a very pleasant sojourn," he finished, somewhat abruptly, and with a comprehensive bow to the party backed away.

But just two months later they ran upon him on the Rhine. The express steamer had picked them up at Bonn and paddled them up the crowded stream to Coblentz, and there at the dock, chatting with two immensely swell Prussian officers, was Mr. Forrest.

"Here's your drummer again, Flo," said Cary, turning disdainfully from the contemplation of the battlements of Ehrenbreitstein. "Just catch on to the cut of those Dutch trousers, will you?" indicating by a nod of his sapient head the tight-fitting, creaseless garments in which were encased the martial lower limbs visible below the long, voluminous skirts of their double-breasted frock-coats. Flo gazed with frank animation in her eyes, but Forrest never saw her until after he had waved adieu to his German friends, standing in statuesque and superb precision at the salute beyond the foaming wake of the Deutscher Kaiser.

"I knew we'd see you again," said Miss Allison, smiling sunshine up into his face, "and I've brought your cap. It's in one of those trunks now," she concluded, indicating the pile of luggage on the deck abaft the wheel. Hubbard and other admirers, who had besieged her on the steamer, were no longer in attendance. In their stead was a well-groomed, sedate, prosperous-looking man referred to as "my father" when Mr. Forrest was presented a moment later, and with him, conversing eagerly and fluently in a high-pitched, querulous voice, was a younger man whose English was as pure as his accent was foreign. "Mr. Elmendorf," said Miss Allison, but she did not explain, as perhaps she might have done, "Cary's tutor." Forrest bowed civilly to both, but looked hard at the latter, and Miss Allison presently went on to explain. "Father joined us nearly a week ago. He couldn't come before. I wish I could have stayed to see the World's Fair, but auntie was so miserable the doctor said she must get away from Chicago at once, and so we had to come. Then Cary's a perfect hoodlum at home,--one scrape after another as fast as he can get in and father can get him out. They sent him with us," she continued, in the flow of her boundless confidences.

"Herr Max is a very highly educated young man, but I don't think he's doing Cary any good."

That night at Mainz there was an episode. Mr. Allison senior, fatigued, had gone to bed as soon as they reached their hotel. Mrs. Lawrence,--"auntie," that is,--Miss Allison, and their maid were billeted in very comfortable rooms under Herr Schnorr's hospitable roof. Elmendorf stepped in to write letters, and Cary sneaked out for a smoke. It was after ten. The shops were closed. Cigarettes had been strictly forbidden, and the boy's small stock of contraband had been discovered and seized that morning at Bonn. Herr Max wrote *currente calamo*, and as he turned off page after page he lost all thought of his charge. Among Cary's treasured possessions was a calibre 32 Smith & Wesson, and with this pellet-propeller in his hip-pocket the boy fancied himself as dangerous as an anarchist. Twice had it been captured by paterfamilias and twice recovered, the last time at Cologne. Carrying concealed weapons was as much against the law in Cologne as it is in Chicago, and much more of an offence, but nothing had there occurred to impel him to draw it. The boat-landing was not five hundred yards away. There under the arching lights of its beautiful bridge, sparkling with the reflection of myriad stars, silently flowed the Rhine, and there lay the Deutscher Kaiser, with her well-stocked larder and wine-room. Thither went the boy in quest of forbidden fruit. A waiter to whom he had confided his desire had promised to have the cigarettes on hand, and kept his promise. For one small package he demanded a four-mark piece,--a silver coin of about the size and rather more than the value of the American dollar. Cary responded with "What you giving us?" which the Teutonic kellner couldn't understand. The boy proffered a mark, the German equivalent for the American quarter, and sought vainly through the misty memories of his lessons for the German equivalent of "Size me up for a chump?" The waiter had friends and fellow-conspirators, the boy had none, and when a grab was made for his portemonnaie he backed against the stone wall and whipped out his pygmy six-shooter. Miss Allison, looking out from her casement over the moonlit beauty of the scene before her, had recognized her brother's form and later his uplifted voice. She knew there was trouble, and felt that worse would follow unless prompt measures were taken. She was not dressed for promenade, being already in *peignoir*, slippers, and dishevelled hair; but the sudden sound of a shot and a scream banished her scruples. She darted into the corridor and on towards the head of the stairs just in time to collide once again with her Atlantic protector, but was not received with open arms. Forrest bade her run back to her room while he sped on to the boy. German police are slow, if sure, but the waiter's associates were quick enough. They had scattered before the police could converge, and Forrest was first at the scene. Just as he supposed, the boy had peppered himself.

It was only a flesh-wound, something to scare and distress and confine Young America to his bed for ten days, and so to be bragged about prodigiously later on. But the injury to German institutions, the affront to the majesty of German law, was not so slight. It took some days of consular and diplomatic correspondence and a week of official espionage to satisfy the local authorities that no deep-rooted conspiracy was at the bottom of this discovery of murderous weapons in the hands of the Amerikaner. In the care of the patient and in all the formalities attendant upon the case, Mr. Forrest proved of infinitely more value than the accomplished tutor. The former, an officer reared with deep regard for established law and order, accepted the situation as a fact, the laws as incontrovertible, and considered himself and friends, although involuntarily, as the offenders. The German-American scholar, on the contrary, spent fruitless hours in striving to argue the officials out of their stand and in preaching a crusade against the laws they were sworn to obey. Forrest won their regard and Elmendorf their distrust, if not disgust, and from the moment Forrest reappeared bearing the limp and lamenting Cary in his arms, Miss Allison had chosen to look upon him as in some sense the family's good angel. They were much together for a week about young Cary's bedside, and the boy swore that if he had "a feller like him for a toot" he wouldn't mind trying to obey. Then, when Forrest had to go his way, she found that she missed him as she never before had missed mortal man. It was the first shadow on her life since her mother's death, five years before.

In September, most unexpectedly, they met him again at Geneva. Cary had been feeding the swans in the blue waters about the little isle of J.J. Rousseau, and was figuring how much he'd have to pay in costs and fines if he yielded to his consuming desire to "drop a donick" on the head of one of them that had spit at him, when Flo suddenly gasped, "Oh! there's----" and stopped short. Loungers and passers-by looked up and shrugged their Gallic shoulders and exchanged glances of commiseration at sight of a sixteen-year-old boy rushing yelling after a cab. But the boy was fleet, despite his recent flesh-wound, and presently reappeared, dragging a man by the arm, who bared his brown head and bowed low over a frankly extended hand. He looked a trifle dusty and travel-stained to Cary's critical eye, and the boy meant to comment on the foreign cut of his Norfolk jacket and knickerbockers, provided a chance were afforded him to enter a remark edgewise, but Florence, with glowing cheeks and sparkling eyes, was pouring forth a volume of welcome and explanation all in one. Forrest was on his way to the station *en route* to Montreux.

"Oh, don't go by rail! Wait and take the boat with us; it's so much lovelier!"

Over at the quay lay moored the Major Davel, and thither Forrest bade the cabman take his luggage. It was indeed lovelier,--the evening voyage up that beautiful Alp-locked lake,--and while auntie, fatigued with her day's shopping and sightseeing, snoozed placidly in the salon, and Cary, on honor not to smoke cigarettes again until his next birthday, was puffing a Swiss "penny-grab" at the bow, Mr. Forrest and this fair, joyous girl sat and talked while the sun went down over the Jura and turned to purple and gold and crimson the dazzling summits of Mont Blanc and the far-away peaks up the valley of the Rhone. Elmendorf was enjoying a week's leave, Mr. Allison was sampling the waters at Carlsbad, and auntie and Florence had Cary on their hands. The boy adored Forrest by this time. Couldn't Forrest spend a day or two? They would take him to Chillon and up to the Rochers de Naye. *There* was a view worth seeing! "I can stand on that point up yonder," said Cary, "a mile and a quarter high, and fire a stone down the chimney of the hotel at Territet." And they did take him, for Forrest remained four days. Mr. Elmendorf wrote that, on the advice of his physician, he had asked for a week more to spend in quiet at his home in the shades of his alma mater in a placid old German town. Stopping at Berne a few hours after leaving his friends on Lac Leman, Mr. Forrest found the quaint old capital crowded. A congress of Socialists had been called, and from all over Europe the exponents of the Order were gathered, and almost the first voice to catch his ear as Forrest strolled through the throng in the open platz near the station was high-pitched, querulous, and oddly familiar. Turning sharply the officer came face to face with Mr. Elmendorf, still presumably recuperating in the shades of the university at Jena; and that night Mr. Elmendorf called upon him at his hotel.

"I found myself so much better," said he, "that I decided to push ahead, and, still availing myself of my leave, to stop and see some of these most interesting old Helvetic cities. My coming here to-day was fortuitous, yet possibly unfortunate. Mr. Allison has a deep-rooted prejudice against anything of this kind,--against anything, I may say, that has a tendency to improve the condition of the laboring man,--and, while I have nothing to shrink from in the matter, I prefer not to offend the sensibilities, whether right or wrong, of my employer, and therefore should, on his account, ask that you make no mention, should you write, of having seen me here." And Elmendorf waited a moment.

"I shall not be apt to write," said Forrest, coldly, after a pause.

"Well--in case you--you see any of the family again. If it's all the same to you----"

"I shall not volunteer any information, Mr. Elmendorf; but should I ever be asked the direct question, since you have nothing to shrink from in the matter, there need be, I presume, no hesitancy in my saying that I saw you here."

"Oh, not at all,--not at all," was the answer, though in tone by no means cheery or confident; and Elmendorf departed with the conviction that Forrest did not like him,--which was simply a case of reciprocity.

There was yet another meeting, as unexpected as its predecessors, between the Allisons and Mr. Forrest, and this was of all perhaps the most decisive. Forrest's leave was soon to expire. He was returning from Vienna to Paris, and met Allison senior at Basle. The Bohemian waters, or the rest and regimen, or both combined, had greatly benefited the merchant. His manner was brisk and buoyant, his face shone with health and content. He was cordiality itself to the man whom he had greeted with but cool civility on the Rhine. "I feel ready for anything," said he, "and am going back at once. Cary and Elmendorf go with me, but Flo and her aunt want to stay awhile in Paris. Look them up, will you, if you go there?--Hotel La-fond." Forrest promised. He was going to Metz and Luxembourg on the way, and purposed spending only a few days in the capital. He found the ladies packing and almost ready to start. Once again he crossed the Atlantic in Miss Allison's company, and this time, though there might have been Hubbards and other gallants aboard, she had no use for them. It was Mr. Forrest's figure her eye sought the moment she came on deck, Forrest's arm on which she leaned in the joyous, exhilarating tramps on the breezy promenade. Every woman on board except Aunt Lawrence believed her engaged to him before they were half-way over, and would have sworn to it at Sandy Hook. Anything more blissful, gladsome, confident than her manner at first could hardly be described, but when it presently began to give way to something half shy, half appealing, almost tender,--when long silences and down-drooping lashes replaced the ceaseless prattle and frankly uplifted eyes,--then there was little room for doubt in Aunt Lawrence's mind that Flo had flung herself away.

"Well, I wash my hands of it," said the pious lady. "It was Fate and her father. He deliberately threw them together again after my warning. Now I suppose he'll have to do something for him, for if Flo loves the man she'll marry him if he hasn't a penny beyond his pay,--which he probably hasn't. There ought to be a law against such things."

But never a confession or confidence did Flo have to offer. The ladies spent a week in New York before going West. Mr. Forrest went on about his business. It was when he met them at Chicago and calmly escorted them from their state-room on the Limited to their waiting carriage that Aunt Lawrence felt the time had come for her to speak; and speak she did the moment Mr. Forrest had closed the carriage door, raised his hat, and was left behind.

"Has that young man asked you to marry him, Florence?"

And Florence burst into tears.

From having been a bitter opponent of the possibility, Mrs. Lawrence from this moment veered squarely around. A month agone she would have resented his daring to speak of such a thing. Now she raged at his daring not to. Here they were home again at Chicago with all Florence's friends crowding about and rejoicing in her return, and here, said Aunt Lawrence, was this extraordinary young man detained on some mysterious duty on the staff of the general commanding, working in his office at the Pullman building by day and meeting Flo at dinners, dances, theatres, and operas by night, coming occasionally to the house, welcomed by her brother, the millionaire, with whom the young man often sat now and had long talks about the questions of the hour, welcomed shyly but unmistakably by Florence, adored by Cary, who took to paying long visits to the lieutenant's workshop and meeting those swells his brother officers, and looked upon with distrust only by Elmendorf and herself. Never before had the lady fancied the tutor or shown a disposition to listen to his dissertations, which were long. Now she rejoiced his soul by encouraging him. It was an easy step to discreet confidences with Forrest as the subject. Mr. Elmendorf became a seeker for truth. Other officers whom Florence met in society came to the house to call, and presently to dine. Mr. Elmendorf and his pupil were seldom absent from the table, and Mr. Elmendorf made martial acquaintances which, as a member of the Allison household, he was welcome to cultivate. One day he came in big with news, and that evening, after a long conference with Elmendorf, Mrs. Lawrence decided on another warning talk with her charming niece.

"Florence," she said, finally, "I am the last woman on earth to pry into any one else's affairs" (a conviction with regard to herself which is cherished by almost every woman), "but I have felt it my duty to learn something about Mr. Forrest's past life. I own I did object to him as a possible suitor, but better that than a man insincere in his intentions. What would you say were I to tell you what I have heard recently?"

Miss Allison turned and faced her aunt unflinchingly, "That he was engaged to Miss Hosmer,--now Mrs. Stuyvesant,--that she broke it off, and that he has never cared for any one since? I know all about it, auntie,--mainly from his own lips."

"Then all I've got to say is, you are the most extraordinary persons I ever met,--*both* of you."

CHAPTER II.

There are many excellent people in this bright world who, like Mrs. Lawrence, are prone to assert that all they've got to say on a given subject is so and so, and then to stultify themselves by proceeding to talk a whole torrent. Mrs. Lawrence said a great deal in the course of this initial interview, and followed it up with a very great deal more. She considered Mr. Forrest's conduct worse than incomprehensible. What business had he to tell a girl his heart was buried in the past and pay her all lover-like attentions in the present? "He hasn't," said Miss Allison, promptly and flatly. "He has simply been kind and friendly. He would have been discourteous, un-American, had he done anything less." It wasn't he who told her he never had cared or would care for any one after Miss Hosmer; Kate Lenox told her that, and so did other girls here. When, then, did Mr. Forrest inform her of his broken engagement? asked Aunt Lawrence. "On the steamer coming home," said Florence. "He couldn't help himself. I met Mrs. Stuyvesant in Washington last winter,--such a lovely woman,--and some one said she was once engaged to an army officer and it was broken off; she found she didn't love him enough to leave her luxurious home to live on the frontier among Indians. I don't know how her name came up, or what prompted me to talk as I did. I was saying that I thought her cruel, heartless, and that she should have considered all that before ever she engaged herself to him; and then he simply put up his hand, saying, 'Do not speak of it, Miss Allison: I was the man.' It fairly took my breath away," said Florence,--which her aunt could hardly believe,--"and I didn't know what to say; and then he went on quietly to speak of her in the most beautiful way, and assured me there were other and graver reasons which led to her decision, some of which, at least, he could not gainsay, and Mr. Stuyvesant's wealth and social position had very little to do with the fact of her finally marrying him, as she did, and not until several years after the engagement was broken."

Indeed, Miss Allison waxed tearfully eloquent in defence of Mr. Forrest, whom she declared high-minded and honorable and manly. He wasn't in love with her, nor she with him,--not a bit; but she honored him and respected him and liked him better than any man she knew, and papa thought him such a superior man, and Cary was devoted to him, and he had been of infinite service to them abroad, and was welcome now and should be welcome any time--any time--to their doors, and if Aunt Lawrence or anybody spoke ill of him to her she'd defend him to the bitter end, and as for hinting or insinuating that he was trifling with her, it was simply outrageous--outrageous, and if Aunt Lawrence dared to let him suppose it was his duty to propose to her now she'd never forgive her,--never. And so Aunt Lawrence discovered that her blithe, merry, joyous niece of the years gone by had developed a fine temper of her own and a capacity for independent thought and action that was simply appalling.

Florence went dancing down into the parlor with flushed cheeks and briny, indignant eyes and the mien of an offended five-foot goddess, leaving Aunt Lawrence to the contemplation of the field of her disastrous defeat and the card of the unworthy object of their discussion:

"What on earth brings him here at this time of day?" quoth she, irate and ruffled. "For a man who is neither lover nor fiance, he assumes the airs and, for aught I know, the rights of both. The girl is as ill-balanced as her mother." And not all women, it must be owned, think too well of an only brother's wife. "The manners of these army men are simply uncouth. Who ever heard of calls at ten A.M.?"

It was but a few minutes before Miss Allison returned. In fact, she did not return to the scene of the late struggle,--a lovely boudoir overlooking the flashing blue waters of the lake from high over the intervening boulevard. Miss Allison went direct to her own rooms on the opposite side of the broad hall-way, and not until evening was Mrs. Lawrence favored with explanation.

"Why are you not dressed?" she somewhat caustically inquired, as her niece came down arrayed for dinner.

For answer Miss Allison contemplated her pretty white arms, and took a backward and downward glance at the fall of the trailing skirt of heavy silk, then--must it be recorded?--she calmly asked, "What's the matter with this?"

"This," said Aunt Lawrence, with marked emphasis, "may do for home dinners, but won't for an opera-party. Here it is seven. You can't change your dress before eight, and you simply can't go to the Langdons' box in that."

"I'm not going to the Langdons' box."

"You were, and Mr. Forrest was to dine here and take you."

"Mr. Forrest left for the West on sudden orders at noon, and came at ten to tell me."

Mrs. Lawrence's hands and eyes went up in mad dismay. "You don't mean to tell me you've given up going because that man's ordered off? Child, child, you are simply bent on ruining yourself socially. I don't wonder people say you're daft about him."

"Who says I'm daft about him?" queried Miss Allison, flushing instantly, but looking dangerous.

"Well, not just that, perhaps," returned Mrs. Lawrence. "But that's what they will say now. Surely Mrs. Langdon could ask somebody in his place who could have escorted you,--or else I could."

"Mrs. Langdon did invite somebody else,--two somebody elses, in fact, as my letter urged her to do. Fanny Tracy was wild to go, and Captain Farwell wild to take her. I did a charitable thing in suggesting them."

"Then the result of that piece of charity will be that all Chicago will say you are so much in love with that man you couldn't go 'Faust' when he went away."

"Chicago has too many other things to think of, and---- Where's papa?" said Miss Allison, turning abruptly from her aunt and moving with quick, impetuous step towards the heavy portiere that hung between the parlor and Mr. Allison's library. But she stopped short at the threshold, for there, just within the rich folds of the hanging barrier, apparently searching for some particular book among the shelves nearest the parlor and farthest from the library lights, and humming musically to himself as he did so, was Cary's tutor.

"I did not know you were here, Mr. Elmendorf," said Miss Allison, coldly. "I supposed you were in the study with my brother."

"I was until a moment ago. We needed a book, and I came down for it."

Mr. Allison's easy-chair and reading-lamp with the evening papers were all arranged as usual, awaiting, at the other end of the room, the coming of the master of the house. It was his custom to read there some hours each evening, and the library was the one room in which he reigned supreme. His books, papers, desks, and tables were sacred to his use, and might not at any time be disturbed by other hands. Even Mrs. Lawrence, who had her own books in her own little snuggery up-stairs, rarely ventured to touch her brother's library shelves. As for Florence, she never cared to. It was well known that Mr. Elmendorf had more than once been sharply rebuked for having helped himself without first seeking the owner's permission. Yet here he was again. The odd thing about it was that this end of the library was dark. The books on these shelves were huge folios, the size of some Brobdingnagian atlas, any one of which required all Mr. Elmendorf's strength to lift from its place. Miss Allison was not over-shrewd. She was frankness, guilelessness itself. She rarely saw through the meanness of man or the duplicity of woman. This, however, was not the first, but the second or third time that Mr. Elmendorf had been revealed behind those curtains when she was in conversation in the parlor, and it dawned upon her at last that Cary's tutor was as good a listener as talker, and there were times when Mr. Elmendorf was fluency itself. He was a shrewd fellow, too, and he read his sentence in her face.

"Miss Allison," said he, quitting his search and stepping boldly forward, "it would be idle in me to disguise, that I have unwittingly heard a portion of the conversation between your aunt and yourself; and, as your brother's friend and tutor, your father's trusted adviser in many a way, both professional and personal,-- indeed, if I may say so without offence, as one who would gladly be your friend,--I feel bound to support Mrs. Lawrence in the view she takes of this--pardon me-- unfortunate matter."

"Mr. Elmendorf!" interrupted Miss Allison, with eyes and cheeks aflame.

"Bear with me one moment," persisted Mr. Elmendorf, with deprecatory gesture. "I am aware that I have not possessed your friendship in the past; indeed, I may say I have been conscious of a distinctly hostile influence; but my devotion to your father and your brother and the interests of the family and all that may affect its good name make it mandatory upon me to speak. I appeal to Mrs. Lawrence to support me in my assertion that I am prompted only by the worthiest motives in thus apparently intrusively, officiously if you will, claiming your attention." Mrs. Lawrence bowed grave assent. She had many a time expressed her disapprobation of Mr. Elmendorf's propensity to interfere in domestic matters wherein he had no concern, but here was a case where unlooked-for support was accorded her side of an unfinished argument. Mrs. Lawrence considered all comment of Mr. Elmendorf on her affairs as utterly unwarrantable, but poor Flo really laid herself open to criticism.

It was Miss Allison who brought matters to a climax. "I refuse to listen," said she, with something very like a stamp of her plump little foot. "Mr. Elmendorf forgets himself entirely when he attempts to--to criticise my conduct."

"Pardon me, Miss Allison, it is not your conduct, it is, on the contrary, Mr. Forrest's, that I consider deserving criticism,--more than criticism. It is of him, not of yourself, that I feel it my duty to speak. I should be disloyal to my employer, to my friends, to my own sense of honor and propriety, were I to keep silence. I know whereof I speak when I say that he is unfit to step within these doors, to presume to address you even as an acquaintance; and if you will but listen----"

"But I won't listen. I forbid your ever daring to speak to me in any such way or on any such subject again." And, so saying, Miss Allison swept angrily from the room.

Elmendorf shrugged his shoulders. "You see," he said, in the high-pitched, querulous tone that so closely resembled a whine, "you see the hopelessness of arguing with a woman in love. I have only succeeded in making another enemy, and my position here will become all the more embarrassing."

"In so far as I can uphold you, Mr. Elmendorf," said Mrs. Lawrence, promptly, "you may count upon me. Flo is stubborn and hot-headed. She looks upon Mr. Forrest as a hero, whereas he is really a detriment to her social future. I rejoice in his being ordered West, and hope the duty will keep him a long time away from Chicago."

"Ah! did he say he was ordered away on any special duty?" asked Mr. Elmendorf.

"I certainly so understood Florence."

Mr. Elmendorf elevated his eyebrows and shrugged his shoulders anew. "That is very unlike the story that was told me at head-quarters," said he, significantly.

"What was that?" asked Mrs. Lawrence, with prompt and pardonable curiosity.

"That he was ordered away--under a cloud--in order to put an end to probable scandal."

"Gambling?" asked Mrs. Lawrence, whose own first-born left college prematurely because of fatal propensities in that line.

"W-e-l-l," answered Elmendorf, pursing up his lips, "I won't say there may not have been something of that kind, but the main trouble is more serious. I speak from excellent authority in saying that the general gave him just sixteen hours in which to pack and start, fixing the noon train to-day as the limit,--very probably to prevent his seeing the--er--woman in the case again."

CHAPTER III.

Miss Allison declined to come down to dinner that night, and Mrs. Lawrence had no power to compel her attendance. What she hoped was that when Mr. Allison came in he would send his mandate; but Mr. Allison did not come. Instead there was a messenger from the club. Mr. Allison was unexpectedly detained by an important meeting of a board of directors, and might not be home until late. The butler made the announcement with his usual impassive face, and Mrs. Lawrence directed dinner served without further delay. When told to summon Master Cary, a servant presently returned with the information that that young gentleman had stepped out. "Slipped out," muttered Elmendorf between his teeth, for no sooner did Cary discover that "dad" was not to be home than he tobogganed down the baluster rail and shot forth into the surrounding darkness, and was blocks away among cronies of his own before his absence was discovered. "My brother is far too lax in his discipline with Cary," said Mrs. Lawrence, in that profound disapprobation which most people have of other people's methods, especially when their own system, or lack of it, has proved conspicuous failure.

"Mr. Allison," said Elmendorf, diplomatically, "is somewhat wedded to his theory, but that may not stand the test of practice. I had flattered myself that the few months of my tuition were beginning to bear good fruit, and that Cary was steadying, so to speak; but ever since the boy began to get this West Point idea into his head I have found him becoming more and more difficult to guide and control. Indeed, while I do not wish to be considered as complaining, I feel bound to say, since you have done me the honor to open the subject, that the influence of Mr. Forrest upon both your nephew and your brother has been detrimental to my usefulness in this household, so much so, in fact, as to prove at times a serious embarrassment."

Now, Mrs. Lawrence had by no means "opened the subject," as intimated by Mr. Elmendorf, but he was adroit in the manipulation of language. He noted unerringly the cloud of dissent in her face, and knew it would find verbal expression provided opportunity were afforded. To head off disclaimer, therefore, he resorted to the time-honored feminine expedient of talking down the other side and giving it no chance to be heard,--an easy matter with him, for when Elmendorf got to talking there was no telling when he would stop or what he might say. He was a man who loved talk for talk's sake, who had an almost maternal fondness for the sound of his own voice, and who petted and cajoled and patted and moulded his phrases and sentences as an indulgent mother might humor a child or a school-girl dress and adorn a doll. Before he had been two months an inmate of the household, old Allison had come to wish he had not begun by prescribing that Cary and his tutor should regularly appear at the family table. Once established there, Elmendorf speedily became dominant. If friends of Miss Allison dropped in to luncheon and the chat was of social matters or other girls, if Allison brought home fellow-magnates to take pot-luck at his hospitable board, if Mrs. Lawrence and her especial cronies discoursed on that never-ending problem, the servants, if Forrest and his army friends came informally, no matter what the subject or who the speakers, Elmendorf speedily "chipped in," as Cary expressed it, and once in could not be driven out. His pet theme was the wrongs of the wage-workers, his pet theory the doctrine of incessant change. His watchword seemed to be "Whatever is is wrong," for against the existing order of things in state, society, or home he was ever ready to wage determined war. Armed with propensities such as these, a profound conviction of his own sense and sagacity and consummate distrust in those of everybody else, it is easy to see that once encouraged to break the ice and join in the current of conversation he could not readily be eliminated. A man of good education was Elmendorf, and during the European trip he had not been so much in the way, but once home again, more and more as the winter wore on did the head of the household find himself wishing he had never set eyes on the man. He heard of him presently as addressing socialistic meetings and appearing prominently at the sessions of the labor unions.

Then in the columns of papers of marked anarchistic tendencies, that had been under the ban ever since the riots of '86, long articles began to appear over his initials, and both in his speeches and in his contributions Elmendorf was emphatic in his condemnation of capital, and in his demands that labor should unite, unite everywhere, and by concerted and persistent effort wring from the congested coffers of capital--Elmendorf loved alliteration--a large share of its hoarded wealth. The hands that wrought the fabric, said he, should share and share alike in every profit. The man who riveted the bolt or swung the hammer deserved equal wage with him whose brain evolved the plan, or whose fortune built the mammoth plant and purchased the costly machinery.

"What I employed him for," said Allison, "was to prepare Cary for college, and to keep him out of mischief; but the boy's running wilder than before. Elmendorf's welcome to his theories, but not to the time they take from the education of my son." It presently transpired that many an evening when they were supposed to be in the study or at the library or the theatre, Elmendorf was off at some meeting of the laboring men, largely attended by loafers who labored not at all, and no one knew just where Cary had gone unless he chose to tell. Elmendorf had long since offended Miss Allison and her friends by intrusion in their talk; he had offended Mrs. Lawrence by comment and criticism on household affairs that were none of his business; he had annoyed Allison by persistence in taking part in the discussion when his business or professional friends happened in. He had time and again thrown down the gauntlet, so to speak, when Forrest or his comrades were present, and challenged the army men to debate as to whether there was the faintest excuse for the existence of even so small a force as ours in a land so great and free; but Forrest coolly--even courteously--refused to be drawn into controversy, and, though treating the tutor with scrupulous politeness, insisted on holding him at a distance. Naturally, therefore, Elmendorf hated the lieutenant and all who trained with him. None the less did he continue making frequent visits to the officers at head-quarters, and there the officers who met him on equal footing at Mr. Allison's table could not snub him. They grew suspicious of him, however, especially after reading his speeches, etc., which as the spring came on grew more and more significant, and so they shut up like so many clams on all professional topics whenever Elmendorf appeared.

For it was well known in the great community that "the regulars" were keeping close watch on the changing phases of what the papers termed "the situation." Twice or thrice before in the history of the city had its mobs overpowered the municipal authority and defied that of the State. Right or wrong, the majority among the prominent citizens believed that in greater force and fury than ever before the turbulent element among the people, taking advantage of some convenient strike, would break bounds once more, and nothing short of disciplined military force would down them. The State troops, vastly improved by the experiences of the past, had won their way to increased confidence and respect, but all the same people took comfort in the thought that only an hour's railway ride away there was posted a compact little body of regulars, and, despite the jealousy aroused in the heart of a free people through the existence of a standing army, it is marvellous to see how much comfort its proximity brings to law-abiding men.

Now, one of Elmendorf's theories, and one upon which he descanted by the hour, was that in the very nature of things it was impossible for people well to do in the world to sympathize with or understand the needs of those who were not so favored. Divine writ, said he, was with him. Just as impossible as for a camel to pass through the needle's eye or for a rich man to enter the kingdom of heaven was it that the wealthy could feel for the poor. Opulence and indigence were no more sympathetic than oil and vinegar. The poor must ever have a champion, a savior, a mediator, or they are ground beneath a relentless heel. It was Elmendorf's belief that no manufacturer, employer, landlord, capitalist, or manager could by any possible chance deal justly with the employed. It was a conviction equally profound that manifest destiny had chosen him to be the modern Moses who was to lead his millions out of the house of bondage. It was astonishing that with purpose so high and aim so lofty he could find time and inclination to meddle with matters so far beneath him; but the trouble with Elmendorf was that he was a born meddler, and, no matter what the occasion, from a national convention to a servants' squabble, he was ever eager to serve as adviser or arbitrator. It was his proclivities in this line that brought on the first clash with Mrs. Lawrence, for in a difference between the lady of the house and the belle of the kitchen, which was, as usual, none of his affair, Elmendorf took sides with the cook. In the light of his conduct on this occasion, Mrs. Lawrence declared him a pest, and she only recanted when thus unexpectedly he arrayed himself under her own banner against her recreant niece.

And so this evening they sat alone in the stately dining-room, and Elmendorf found in Mrs. Lawrence an eager and even sympathetic listener, for just so soon as the services of the butler could be dispensed with the tutor opened fire on Forrest and his alleged iniquities, and from this as entering wedge he found it easy to favor the aunt with his views as to what should be done towards reclaiming the niece, so lamentably and notoriously infatuated.

Mrs. Lawrence winced. It is all very well for a woman to say such things herself in the heat of argument and to the object of her wrath, but quite another matter to hear them applied by somebody else, and that somebody a dependent, so to speak, in the household. Mrs. Lawrence, it may be remembered, was indignant at Forrest first because she thought he meant to offer himself to Florence, and then because she thought he didn't. She did not want Florence to marry him, but still less did she want that he should not want her. That was unbearable. She upbraided Florence for seeing so much of Forrest, because it made people think her in love with him, and she raged at the people who dared to think as she said they did. Mrs. Lawrence, therefore, may with safety be set down as somewhat inconsistent.

"I do not think my niece is at all infatuated with Mr. Forrest, Mr. Elmendorf," said she, somewhat severely. "She admires him greatly, and there happens to be no one else to occupy her thoughts just now. I beg you, therefore, to dismiss that idea at once and for all time."

"I should be glad to do so, Mrs. Lawrence," replied the tutor, with much gravity, "and could do so, perhaps, were it not that you yourself gave me, in the conversation I was so unfortunate as accidentally to overhear, the confirmation. Would it not be better now, instead of working at cross-purposes in this matter, if you were to trust me more fully and enable me to act in harmony with your plans and wishes? I shrink from intruding unasked, but, believe me, I too have heard such talk as convinces me that it is high time Miss Allison's friends took counsel together to protect her good name."

Indignant, as most women would be, at being reminded of her own responsibility for a false impression, Mrs. Lawrence could have found it easy to put an end to the conference then and there, but for Elmendorf's adroit reference to "other talk." That piqued her curiosity and held her.

"What talk? Where?" she asked.

"I do not like to mention names, Mrs. Lawrence. My acquaintance among the officials at head-quarters has become extensive, and much is said in confidence to me that perhaps wouldn't be heard in their chat with others. Indeed, I may say that some among the more thoughtful and broad-minded of their number--there are a few such--have sought my views upon important questions of the day and have favored me with their opinions."

"And do you mean that Florence has been discussed there, among all those men,--those officers?" interrupted Mrs. Lawrence, with justifiable wrath.

Elmendorf shrugged his shoulders. "Of course I ought not to betray my hosts or give away their secrets, but do you suppose that there, any more than among the loungers of the clubs, a woman's name is never discussed?"

"I thought they prided themselves on being gentlemen," said Mrs. Lawrence, wrathfully; "and gentlemen would never permit it."

"Ah, my dear madam, there's the trouble. A man is not necessarily a gentleman because wealth and social position impel him to membership in one of these forcing-houses of luxurious iniquity we call clubs, or because four years in a West-Point monkey-jacket win him a commission as a genteel loafer. A woman's name is held far less in reverence among them than it is among the humblest of our masses. Oh, yes, I anticipate your question," said he, at this juncture, with deprecatory gesture and faint, significant smile. "True, I am not personally a member of any of those clubs, nor do I wish to be, but I know men and mingle with them elsewhere,--everywhere else, in fact. The roof of the club-house cloaks their misdeeds, and worse things are said and done beneath it than outside. As for officers, the only reason why there is apt to be a stronger percentage of common decency among them is that they are chosen from the masses of the people and sent to the Point simply to be moulded, not reformed. Mr. Forrest is an example of the so-called blue-blooded stock. His people are 'swells,' so to speak,--people whose heads are held very high and their morals correspondingly low,--people who think it condescension on their part to notice wage-workers except as menials. Hence I am in no wise surprised to hear of him as I do, even among those who are--well, of his own cloth."

"Surely, Mr. Elmendorf, the officers who have so often dined here do not entertain ill opinions of Mr. Forrest. Such men as Colonel Kenyon, Captain Waring,

Major Cranston,--they have known him long and well, and they speak of him, to us at least, most highly."

Again the significant shrug of Elmendorf's shoulders and the sneer in his tone. "Oh, certainly," said he. "***Noblesse oblige***, or honor among thieves, whichever maxim you choose. I doubt not that in his younger days each of the eminently respectable trio you mention was no more a model of morality than is Mr. Forrest. I have, indeed, heard as much of Captain Waring; but one has only once to penetrate beyond the veil of that professional reserve which they assume, and the details of one another's lives are not such guarded secrets, after all."

"And you really mean that from them--among them you have learned these--these----"

"These particulars of Mr. Forrest's sudden orders to leave the city?" said Elmendorf, dryly, with another shrug. "From where else? Even to the name and station of the lady in the case."

CHAPTER IV.

Not half a mile away from the Allisons' costly residence was the home of Major Cranston, an officer of some thirty years' experience in the cavalry. It was an unpretentious, old-fashioned frame house, that had escaped the deluge of fire that swept the city in '71, and that looked oddly out of place now in the midst of towering apartment blocks or handsome edifices of brick and stone. But Cranston loved the old place, and preferred to keep it intact and as left to him at the death of his father until such time as he should retire from active service. Then he might see fit to rebuild. The property was now of infinitely more value than the house. "You could move that old barrack out to the suburbs, cut down them trees, and cut up the place into buildin'-lots and sell any one of them for enough to build a dozen better houses," said a neighbor who had prospered, as had the Cranstons, by holding on to the paternal estate. But Cranston smilingly said he preferred not to cut up or cut down. "Them" trees and he had grown up together. They were saplings when he was a boy, and had grown to sturdy oakhood when his own youngsters, plains-bred little cavaliers, used to gather their Chicago friends about them under

the whispering leaves and thrill their juvenile souls with stirring tales of their doings "out in the Indian county." Louis Cranston was believed to have participated
with his father's troop in many a pitched battle with the savage foe before his tenth
birthday, and "Patchie," the younger, was known to be so called not because of his
mother's having sprung from the distinguished family in which George Patchen
was a patron saint, but because he had been born in the Arizona mountains and
rocked in a Tonto cradle. Those two boys were now stalwart men, cattle-growers in
the Far West, whose principal interest in Chicago was as a market for their branded
steers. They had their own vines and fig-trees, their own wives and olive-branches,
and after the death of the venerable grandparents the homestead on the shores of
Lake Michigan was for some years untenanted.

But therein were stored the old furniture and the old books and pictures, all
carefully guarded by one of Cranston's veteran sergeants, who, disabled by wounds
and infirmities, was glad to accept his commander's offer to give to him and his a
home and suitable pension in return for scrupulous care of the old place. At long
intervals the master had come in on leave, and the neighbors always knew when
to expect him, for the snow-shovel or the lawn-mower, holly wreaths or honey-
suckles, seemed to pervade the premises, and old McGrath's neatest uniform was
hung out to sun and air on the back piazza. Mac was a bibulous veteran at times,
a circumstance of which place-hunters were not slow to take advantage on those
rare occasions of the owner's home-coming, and many a time did the major receive confidential intimation from the Sheehans, Morriseys, and Meiswinkles in
service in the neighborhood that McGrath was neglectful of his patron's premises
and over-given to the flowing bowl; but in Mrs. McGrath's stanch protectorate, as
in McGrath's own fidelity, Cranston had easy confidence. Twenty years of close
communion all over the frontier give fair inkling as to one's characteristics, and
Cranston had known Mac and his helpmeet even longer. "Dhrink, yer honor? Faith
an' I do, as regularly as iver I drunk the captain's health and prosperity in the ould
regiment; and I'd perhaps be doin' it too often, out of excessive ghratitude, but for
Molly yonder. She convinces me wid me own crutch, sorr." And Molly confirmed
the statement: "I let him have no more than is good for him, major, barrin' Patrick's
Day and the First of April, that's Five Forks,--when he always dhrinks as many fingers at a time. Then he's in arrest till Appomattox, nine days close,--and then I let

him out for a bit again. Never fear, major, I'm the dishbursin' officer of the family, an' the grocer has his orders." Mac had his other anniversaries, be it understood, on all of which occasions he repaired to Donnelly's Shades on a famous thoroughfare two blocks west of the Cranstons' back gate, and entertained all comers with tales of dragoon days that began in the 50's and spread all over the century. Shrewd historians of the neighborhood made it a point to look up the dates of Brandy Station and Beverly Ford, of Aldie, Winchester, and Waynesboro', of Yellow Tavern and Five Forks, as well as to keep tab on subsequent events of which history makes no mention, but which troopers know well, for Summit Springs, Superstition Mountain, Sunset Pass, and Slim Buttes--a daring succession of sibilant tongue-tacklers--were names of Indian actions from Dakota to the Gila the old soldier loved to dwell upon, even if Donnelly's whiskey had not put clogs on his tongue. Two things was Mac always sure of at the Shades,--good listeners and bad liquor; but the trooper who has tasted every tipple, from "pine-top" to mescal, will forgive the latter if sure of the former. Donnelly had his "ordhers," as Mrs. Mac said. The sergeant was to be accorded all respect and credit, and a hack to fetch him home when his legs got as twisted as his tongue: Mrs. McGrath would be around within forty-eight hours to audit and pay the accounts. Donnelly sought to swindle the shrewd old laundress at the start, and thereby lost Mac's valuable custom for six long and anniversary-laden months. Then he came to terms, and didn't try it again for nearly two years, which was remarkable in a saloon-man. This time Donnelly was forgiven only upon restitution of the amount involved and the presentation to Mrs. McGrath of a very ornate brooch in emeralds and brilliants--or something imitative thereof--representing the harp of Erin. From this time on things had gone smoothly.

A wonderful woman was Mrs. Mac, as her husband never failed to admit. She had slaved and saved for him in a score of garrisons. They had their little hoard carefully invested. They hired a young relative and countryman to do the hard work about the premises, and they guarded every item of the major's property with a fidelity and care that knew no lapse, for Mrs. Mac was never so scrupulous as when her lord was in his cups. "No," said Cranston, when a neighbor once asked him if he wasn't afraid of serious losses through Mac's occasional inebriety. "The more he drinks the stricter her vigilance, and she's the smarter of the two."

But there came a time when the major found it necessary to caution Mrs. Mac, and that was when it was brought to his ears that McGrath's nephew, the young Irish helper above referred to, was a frequent attendant at certain turbulent meetings held over on the west side, where he had been seen drunk on two occasions. "It's one thing to allow an old soldier like Mac his occasional indulgence," said Cranston; "he was started that way, and he never becomes riotous or ugly; but there is no excuse for the boy. Those meetings alleged to be held in the interests of the workingmen are attended mainly by tramps and loafers, fellows who couldn't be hired to do a day's honest work, and are addressed by professional demagogues who have no end but mischief in view. You saw what resulted here when you first came in, seven years ago. I don't want to hurt Mac's feelings by saying he's a bad example to his nephew, and I don't want to let him know where the boy has been spending his evenings. He'd break every bone in the youngster's skin if he thought he was consorting with anarchists and rioters; and I tell you because you couldn't have heard of it or you yourself would have taken the boy in hand."

"Taken him in hand, sorr? I'd 'a' broke the snow-shovel over the scandalous back av him if I'd heerd a worrd av it. He's aff to-day sparkin' the girls in the block beyant, but I'll wait for him to-night. Thank ye, sorr, for not tellin' Mac. It's his own poor sister's boy, an' like his own that was tuk from us at Apache, but Mac would kill him before he'd have him trainin' wid them Dutchmen and daygoes." (Mrs. McGrath did not share Mulvany's views that "There are Oirish and Oirish." Even Phoenix Park had failed to shake her view that anarchy and assassination belonged only to "foreigners." No Irishman, said she, was in the bloody bomb business of '86; and as for Dr. Cronin, that was a family matther entirely.) "But if Tim's been goin' to meetin' wid the like av them, he's been misguided by them as knows betther. Savin' your presence, major, what would the gentleman be doin' wid him that was here last week?"

Cranston looked at his housekeeper in surprise. "The gentleman who came to look over my books?--Mr. Elmendorf?"

"The same, sorr. He came three times while the major was away, and Tim was forever sayin' what a fine, smart man he was for a foreigner, and how he was for helpin' the poor man."

Cranston gave vent to a long whistle of surprise and sudden enlightenment. "When was Mr. Elmendorf last there?" he presently inquired.

"All last week, sorr; three times at least I let him into the library as usual, but he only stayed there awhile. He was talkin' outside wid Tim an hour."

The major turned away in deep thought. Only two months before, ordered from the Far West to take station at the new post near the city, he had met El- mendorf when dining at the Allisons'. The next morning he found him at head- quarters, chatting affably with the aides-de-camp, and later he encountered him at Brentano's. Just how it came about Cranston could not now remember, but he had invited Elmendorf to step in and look over some old books of his father's, and as the tutor became enthusiastic he was bidden to come again. Out at the post the major established his modest soldier home, much missing the companionship of his devoted wife, who was in Europe at the time with their only daughter. Every week, perhaps, he would run in for half a day to look over his possessions, but meantime he had given Elmendorf authority to make a complete catalogue of the books, as well as to make himself at home in the library, a room which Mrs. McGrath kept in apple-pie order. But the fame of Elmendorf had spread from the city to the gar- rison, and Cranston had already begun to wish he had been less impulsive in his invitation, when Mrs. Mac told him of the missionary work being done among his retainers by this stranger within his gates. The question now was, what action could be justifiably taken?

Entering the old dimly-lighted study, long sacred to his father's use and now sacred to his memory, the major found on every hand evidences that Elmendorf had indeed been at work. Out from their accustomed places on the shelves the books had been dragged, and were now stacked up about the room in perplexing disarray. Some lay open upon the table, others on the desk near the north win- dow, his father's favorite seat, and here some of the rarest of the collection were now piled ten and fifteen deep. On the table in loose sheets were some pencilled memoranda on names, authors, and dates of publication. On the desk were several pads or blocks of the paper much used by writers for the press, and, face upward, among them, held by an old-fashioned glass paper-weight, were a dozen leaves closely pencilled in Elmendorf's bold hand. Cranston raised the weight, expecting to find some more memoranda concerning his precious books, but was not entirely surprised to read, in glaring head-lines, "The Wage-Worker's Weapon," followed by some vehement lines denunciatory of capital, monopoly, "pampered palates in palatial homes, boodle-burdened, beer-bloated legislators," etc., the sort of alliterative and inflammatory composition which, distributed in the columns of the papers of the *Alarm* and *Arbeiter Zeitung* stamp, was read aloud over the evening pipes and beer to knots of applauding men, mostly tramps and idlers, in a thousand groggeries throughout the bustling city. Cranston lifted the file from the desk as though to read beyond the first sheet, but on second thought replaced it. Something about the "threatening bayonets of Federal hirelings" at the foot of the first page promised lively developments farther on, and recalled vividly the editorials in similar strain that had been brought to the attention of the officials at head-quarters, more than one of whom had expressed the belief that they could spot the author on sight. Cranston turned from it in some disgust, and resumed the contemplation of the work already done. All he expected--all he had stipulated for--was a catalogue of the books,--something he himself had not had time to make, and a "job" which, to a man of scholarly tastes and education upon whose hands time was apparently hanging heavily and that equivalent of time, money, hanging not at all, would prove agreeable and acceptable. Cranston's father loved those books, and had grouped them on his shelves according to their subjects, history, art, science, the drama, the classics, standard fiction, and modern literature having received each its allotted space, and not for a heavy reward would the son have changed them; but here already were more than half these prized possessions tumbled promiscuously all over the room, and the soldier could have sworn in hearty trooper fashion over the disarray, but for the silent presence of his mother's portrait above the mantel facing the father's desk. He had heard only recently of the tutor's avowed proclivities for tearing down and stirring up the existing order of things, and here was conclusive evidence that the gifted Elmendorf proposed the complete rebuilding on his own lines of the fabric that was the revered father's happiest work, even while incidentally devoting some hours each day to stirring up a similar overturning in society. That Elmendorf was not destitute of practical business views, however, may be made apparent from the fact that when Cranston had intimated a desire to have him name the sum he would consider a fair compensation for the work, intending then to add a liberal percentage to the estimate, the scholar replied that it would have to depend upon the number of days and hours it took from other avocations, and it was now evident that a long engagement was in contemplation.

Closing the door after him and bidding Mrs. McGrath allow no one to enter the study until his return unless Mr. Elmendorf should come in, Major Cranston went in search of him. It was barely noon, up to which hour he was supposed to be closeted with his pupil at the Allisons' home. Then after a light luncheon it was his wont to sally forth on a tramp, Cary starting, but rarely returning, with him. When Cranston was at head-quarters a fortnight previous, the officers were speaking of the almost daily appearance about two o'clock of Mr. Elmendorf, who was possessed with a desire to get into the general's office and impress that magnate with his views concerning the impending crisis. The general, however, being forearmed, was always too busy to accord the interview, one experience having proved more than enough. Everybody was beginning to give Elmendorf the cold shoulder there, and by this time, reasoned Cranston, he must have had sense enough to discontinue his visits. Here, however, he underrated Elmendorf's devotion to his principles, for such was the tutor's conviction of their absolute wisdom and such his sense of duty to humanity that he was ready to encounter any snub rather than be balked in his determination to right the existing wrongs. Cranston did not want to go to the Allisons' and ask for Elmendorf. He had that to say which could not be altogether pleasant and was altogether personal, and he had no right to carry possible discord into a fellow-citizen's home. The Lambert Library, a noble bequest, stood within easy range of Allison's house and his own, a sort of neutral ground, and from there did Cranston despatch a special messenger with a note.

"Will Mr. Elmendorf kindly drop in at the Lambert Library when he has finished luncheon? I have to take the three P.M. train back to Sheridan, and desire five minutes' conversation relative to affairs at the study as I found them this morning," was all the major wrote, but it was nearly half-past one before that boy returned with the answer. There was no telephone at the Allisons', for the millionaire had long since ordered it out, finding his home peace broken up by incessant summonses from all manner of people. Cranston waited impatiently, and meant to upbraid the boy. "It wasn't my fault, sir: the gentleman was at lunch and wouldn't write until he had finished," was the explanation. Cranston tore open the unexpected reply:

"Mr. Elmendorf deeply regrets that an important engagement in a distant quarter of the city will render it impossible to meet Major Cranston as proposed. If the major will kindly write his suggestions they will receive all consideration and prompt acknowledgment."

"And it had taken Elmendorf," said Cranston, wrathfully, "at least three-quarters of an hour to concoct that palpable dodge."

The railway station was a mile away, and he had several matters to attend to. It was one of his weaknesses that when he had a thing to say and meant to say it, delay was a torment. The librarian was a man whom he knew well. "Mr. Wells, I've got to write quite a letter and do it quick," said he, entering the office. "Can I impose upon your good nature here?"

"Why, certainly, major. Miss Wallen will type it for you as fast as you can talk it," said the librarian, rising and indicating a slender girl who was bending busily over her typewriter.

"Oh, I didn't mean that," the major began; "and yet I don't know, I've sometimes had to dictate reports. The only thing is, I shouldn't care to hurt a man's feelings by letting him see that somebody else knew of the matter; yet I'll want to keep a copy, for I've got to give him a rasping."

"Miss Wallen can write a dozen copies at once, if you wish," said Wells; "and as for hurting anybody's feelings, nobody could extract a word from her on the subject."

"Then if the young lady will be so kind," said Cranston, bowing courteously, "I should be most glad to avail myself." Making no reply, the girl deftly fitted the sheets to the roller and waited expectant. "Don't go, Mr. Wells. I assure you there is no need," said Cranston, as the librarian started to leave the room.

"I've got to; it's my dinner-hour. Miss Wallen goes at twelve, and I after her return. If there's anything the office can do for you, don't hesitate to ask." And with that he was gone.

Miss Wallen's slim white hands were poised in readiness. "Chicago, June--, 1894," began the major. There was an instant of swift-clicking keys and a pause for more. "June--, 1894," repeated Cranston.

"Yes, sir, I have that."

"Already? I didn't suppose it could be done so fast. Do I give you the address now?"

"If you please."

"Mr. Max Elmendorf," he began. "Shall I spell it for you?"

The swift fingers faltered. Some strange sudden cloud overshadowed the bright intelligent face. The girl turned abruptly away a moment, then suddenly arose and hastened to the water-cooler under the great window across the room. Keeping her back resolutely towards the visitor, she swallowed half a glass of water, then presently resumed her seat. "Excuse me," she said. "I am ready now."

"You found the heat very trying, I fear," said the major. "Pray do not attempt this if you are tired after your walk. It can wait as well as not."

"It is something that doesn't have to be done to-day?" she asked, looking quickly up.

"Certainly not, if the sun has been too much for you. Has it?"

No answer for a moment. "It isn't the sun," finally replied Miss Wallen, "but I--should rather not take this."

CHAPTER V.

That evening as Major Cranston was getting into uniform again and pondering not a little over the odd behavior of Mr. Wells's stenographer, the young lady in question, her day's library duties at an end, was walking thoughtfully homeward. She chose a route that carried her close to the dancing waters of the lake. It was a longer way, but she loved it and the fresh, cool wind sweeping inland from the seemingly boundless sheet of blue. She was a slender girl, rather above the medium height, a girl with dark earnest eyes and heavy coils of brown, lustrous hair, and a grave, sweet face, whereon already there were traced indelibly lines that told of responsibility and work and care. She dressed simply, inexpensively, yet with a certain style that well became the willowy grace of her figure. She moved swiftly, but without apparent effort. She walked well, bore herself well, and sped along on her homeward way as though absorbed in her thoughts, except when occasionally glancing out over the sparkling expanse to her right. Other women, and nurse-maids with romping children, dawdled about the sunny foot-path along the breakwater; Miss Wallen alone seemed walking with definite purpose. Nearly opposite the Grant Memorial the roadway swept close by the path, and here it became necessary for her to cross to the western side. Carriages were rolling almost ceaselessly by, and, seeing her waiting an opportunity, a Park policeman signalled to the drivers of those nearest at hand and beckoned to the girl to come on. She obeyed, somewhat timidly glancing about her. One carriage, drawn by spirited bays, had too much headway, and was well upon the crossing before the coachman could help it. It brought her almost face to face with the occupants, and for an instant hid her from the sight of the friendly policeman. When she disappeared, her eyes were downcast, her features placid, even a little pale; when, an instant later, he again caught sight of her, Miss Wallen's eyes were flashing and her soft cheeks aflame. A man in the carriage sitting opposite two ladies, one of middle age and dignified bearing, the other young and divinely fair, had seemed suddenly to recognize her and whipped off his hat in somewhat careless fashion. Taking no notice whatever of the salutation beyond coloring vividly, Miss Wallen passed quickly behind the carriage and was speedily over the crossing.

"A friend of yours, Mr. Elmendorf?" asked the elder lady, languidly.

"A friend of--Mr. Forrest's, rather," was the significant reply, and both ladies started, the younger turning to see who it could be, the elder staring one instant after her, then suddenly confronting Elmendorf again. One swift glance at her niece, and Mrs. Lawrence, with uplifted eyebrows, framed her question with sensitive, speechless lips. Elmendorf nodded sapiently. Then Miss Allison turned around.

"What's her name? Who is she?"

"Her name is Wallen. She is employed at the Lambert Library."

"Oh, indeed!" exclaimed Miss Allison, in quick and lively interest. "I've heard Mr. Forrest speak of her. I do wish we could see her again." Whereupon Mrs. Lawrence and Mr. Elmendorf exchanged glances of commiseration.

A quarter of a mile farther up the drive Mr. Elmendorf checked the driver. "If you will excuse me now, ladies, I have a call to make near here, and will leave you. Should Cary return before I do, kindly ask him not to go out again until I see him."

Mrs. Lawrence suggested driving him to his destination, but Elmendorf declined. Two minutes more, and he had disappeared from their view among the shrubbery, and in ten was rapidly walking southward along a busy thoroughfare. Just as he expected, coming up the opposite side of the street, moving swiftly and with downcast eyes, was Miss Wallen. Springily he crossed, and the next instant was lifting his hat in more respectful fashion than when in the park, half confront-ing, half turning as though to join her. Barely noticing him at all, Miss Wallen moved determinedly on, and Elmendorf, following, placed himself at her side.

"I could not but note your manner to me yesterday in the library, Miss Wallen, and indeed on several previous occasions, and in spite of it I venture to ask you to listen patiently to me for a moment. My object is such as to entitle my words to your respect, not resentment. It is for your own sake, your mother's, your name, that I brave your indignation again."

"If it is to repeat what you intimated the other day, Mr. Elmendorf," said the girl, in low, firm tone, "I refuse to listen. You have no right to speak in such a way."

"I have the right to try and save a poor girl from fatal error. I have devoted the best years of my life to the cause of the poor as against the rich, the down-trodden against the purse-proud. I should not have presumed to speak to you on such a sub-ject had I not heard your name lightly, slightingly used among these very satraps whom Mr. Forrest hails as companions,--comrades. It is to protect you from the misjudgment, the censure of others that I strive to warn you. Pardon me if I recall to you that it was partially, at least, on my recommendation that you were given the position at the library, and that now my name as your endorser is measurably involved. Of course if after what I have to say you persist in receiving Mr. Forrest's--attentions, as we will call them, you must do so at your own risk."

"Mr. Elmendorf, I have told you that there is no truth whatever in these re-ports."

"I do not say there is. It is to warn you of the scandalous, outrageous things these people in so-called high society say of people who are in humbler walks of life that I ventured to relate what I'd heard. It is to obviate the possibility of them in future."

"I have told you, Mr. Elmendorf, that I need no such warning, that I will listen to no such affront. I refuse to believe that any gentleman of Mr. Forrest's set has spoken ill of me. I know none of them, they know nothing of me."

"Knew nothing, perhaps, until your name became linked with his,--how," said he, with significant shrug of his shoulders, "I know not, unless he himself has boy-ishly boasted of----"

But here Miss Wallen stopped short and faced him. "I will hear no more of this, either now or hereafter," she said, with blazing eyes, then turned abruptly, and entered the hall-way of an apartment-house close at hand and shut the door in his face. It was not her home, as Elmendorf knew very well, but possibly friends lived there who would give her refuge and welcome. At all events, he had received his *conge*, and there was nothing for it but to go; and go he did, in high dudgeon. Not until Miss Wallen, watching from an upper window in the room of a friend and fellow-worker, had seen him board a car and disappear with it far down the street, did she resume her homeward walk; and now her eyes were wet with indignant tears.

That Mr. Elmendorf should have asserted that it was through his influence, "partially, at least," Miss Wallen had received her appointment in the library was characteristic of Mr. Elmendorf. Coming to the city himself a stranger, only the year previous, he had spent some hours there each day in reading and writing and study, and had early made acquaintance with Mr. Wells, the librarian, greatly impressing that gentleman at first with the fluency of his chat and the extent of his travel, information, and culture. John Allison, millionaire and manager, was one of the trustees of the Lambert bequest, and when Cary came home from boarding-school in April--a premature appearance which the superintendent's letter fully explained--Allison didn't know what to do with him. "I wish I knew the right sort of tutor to take him in hand," said he to Wells, and Elmendorf, apparently deep in a volume across the office, heard, and promptly acted upon the hearing. He asked Wells for a letter of introduction and recommendation. Wells, having known the applicant less than a fortnight, was pleased with him and said what he could. Allison was impressed by the applicant's fluency and apparent frankness, and in less than a week the erudite Elmendorf found himself in halcyon waters. Then came the foreign trip, another thing to rejoice in; but before he sailed Elmendorf had had an opportunity of doing good to his kind, as he conceived it. Seeking an inexpensive lodging on his arrival in Chicago, he had found a neat, cheerful home under the roof of an elderly widow, a Mrs. Wallen, in a little house on the north side. She lived alone with her daughter, who, it presently transpired, was her main support. There was a son, a stalwart fellow, too, who, being only twenty-four and a man of some education and ability, should have been the mother's prop and stay in her declining years, and so he would have been, very possibly, but for the fact that he had provided himself with encumbrances of his own in the shape of a wife, two children, and numerous debts. He was provident in no other way. "Martin," as the mother fondly said, "would have made a mark in the world if he'd only been started right," but as Mart started himself he started wrong. So long as the father lived, both brother and sister had been well educated and gently reared, for Mr. Wallen was a man of scholarly tastes, but a poor man slaving on a poor man's salary. He had little to leave his children beyond his blessing and the care of their aging mother. Martin was already pledged to a girl schoolmate when the father died, and Jeannette, his sister, who seemed to be the only practical member of the household, promptly withdrew from school, invested her savings in a typewriter, spent her days in the care of her mother and the little house, two rooms in which were presently advertised as to let furnished, went to evening school at a business school, practised stenography and typewriting when not doing housework, washing dishes, or making clothes for her mother and herself, and patiently, pluckily, cheerily looked forward to the time when Mart could help. Mart spent six months "hunting for something to suit," and found nothing he liked so much as making love to his pretty, penniless neighbor. The clerkships he was offered didn't pay twenty dollars a week, which was the least he thought a man of his ability and education should accept. Jeannette told him the proper way was to take ten if he could get it, and work his way up; but Mart disapproved of women's interference in his affairs. It ended in his finally getting a bottom-of-the-list berth in the freight depot of a big railway, and a wife forthwith. Jeannette said nothing. She had taken Mart's measure and saw this coming. "If I do not soon have to take care of Mart's wife and babies, I'll be in luck," was the thought that possibly occurred to her; but she was a silent little body, much given to shrewd and common-sense observation of the world in which she lived. She was a sunny-natured, merry-hearted child in the old days, and even as she grew older and more burdened with care the little home still echoed to the sound of her blithe song as she flitted from room to room about her work, ever brave, hopeful, uncomplaining. "If I only had Jenny's spirits," said the widow to her one lodger, "I might do something, too," but, as she hadn't Jenny's spirits or disposition, by a good deal, the bereaved lady thought it unnecessary to try. It was Jenny who bore the burden of every detail, Jenny who did their humble marketing, Jenny who made the hard bargains with landlord and coal-merchant, Jenny who taught and supervised the one clumsy damsel who was brought in as cook, scullion, laundress, and maid-of-all-work, and Jenny who, after all, did more than she taught. It was Jenny who cut and fashioned almost every garment worn by either her mother or herself, who made and trimmed the modest little hats or bonnets, who watched the bargain-counters at the great retail shops and wished that women didn't have to wear gloves and buttoned boots; Jenny who had to follow up their flitting lodgers,--young men who folded their tents like the Arabs they were, and as silently stole away out of the house, leaving sometimes a big lodging-bill and little luggage; Jenny who presently had to nurse Mart's wife and baby, just as she expected, for Mart lost that job, and the house he had rented, and the furniture he hadn't paid for and that was seized just when most needed. So baby Number One first saw the light under the roof that Jenny's hard work paid for,--a lodger having opportunely "skipped." And all the while she managed to keep up her study and practice, and to do little odd jobs in copying, sitting far into the dawn sometimes with aching arms and wrists and burning eyes and whirling brain. There was no yielding to "beauty sleep" for poor Jenny. Dark circles often settled underneath the brave, steadfast eyes, and big, blinding tears sometimes welled up from unseen depths when no one was near to spy upon her woman's weakness, and the very people she slaved for were often querulous and complaining, and Mart's wife had about as much helpfulness as a consumptive old cow. Jenny had to tell Mart he must find work and pay their board, or some portion of it, and Mart got another berth at another railway depot, and, without paying anything whatever for the months he and his had lived under the mother's roof, or much for the new furniture, moved into another house, where the family circle was presently reinforced by the coming of another baby. Meantime, however, Jenny's skill, quickness, and accuracy had been steadily bringing her work into favor. A girl friend and fellow-student had a good position in a down-town office, where lawyers and business-men brought many a long paper demanding immediate copies, and thither Jenny moved her typewriter, shrewdly calculating that the money she could earn would more than offset the expense of a good servant at home. As for car-fare, she meant to walk: she needed exercise. As for luncheon, she'd carry it with her in her little basket. The plan worked well. There were some days and weeks in which she was given as much as she could possibly finish, but there were others--alack! many others--when nothing came. There was a winter when she wore old clothes, a winter through which other young women in the great hive of a business block were blooming in gowns and garments that were of latest mode and material. It was, so far as work was concerned, either a feast or a famine with her, and she longed for just such a position as that held by an older scholar, who was stenographer and typewriter on salary in the office of a great law firm and yet was enabled to take frequent transcribing or copying from outside; but for a billet of this kind she looked in vain. Then came another winter. How it affected Miss Wallen can best be told through this simple fact, that she was no longer able to ride home even in the dark wet evenings. Mart had again been turned out of house and home, and came with his ailing wife and wailing babies to the doting mother's door, and again was Jenny burdened with their maintenance. Mart had struck. There had been a scaling down of wages for all hands. Most of them, realizing that these were hard times and that other and better were coming, stood by the company. Mart was a leader at the meetings of the employees, and a brilliant orator. With all the eloquence of which he was capable he urged his fellows to stand together and strike. He was one of a committee of five sent to see the local manager. The manager showed the facts, and the other men were satisfied that things were about as he showed. They had been long in his employ, and Mart but a short time. The manager addressed himself to the old men, rather ignoring the new, and Mart's tongue and temper got away with him. He said he'd strike anyhow, and he did. He struck his own name off the company's books.

And so during these dark, dreary winter evenings, sometimes wet and raw, sometimes bitterly cold, quitting when she could her desk at five o'clock, yet often kept pegging away until later, Miss Jeannette Wallen walked those crowded blocks below the State Street bridge and all the many, many squares that interposed between her and her little home. As the days began to lengthen and the cold to strengthen, she sometimes reached there well-nigh frozen and exhausted, to be welcomed and regaled not so much with hot tea and loving words as by wailing infants and complaining women,--Mart being, as usual, away at some soul-stirring meeting, where much was said about the wrongs of the workingman, but nothing thought of those of the workingwoman.

And then came an adventure. Many a time had she been accosted by street prowlers, and sometimes followed, but her rule had been to make no reply, simply to walk straight on, and look neither to the right nor to the left. One dark evening in early January she had been working late, and it was nearly seven as she passed the river. A few blocks farther north she overtook a man whose unsteady gait did not prevent his quickening speed and striving in turn to overtake her. Finding him at her heels and his detaining hand actually on her arm, her nerve gave way, and she took to flight, her pursuer following. Half a block ahead and around a corner was the apartment-house where she had acquaintances, and into the hall-way Jenny bolted, hoping to turn and slam the door into the blackguard's face, but, to her horror, the heavy portal refused to swing. Despairingly she touched the electric button, then turned pluckily to face her pursuer and warn him off. But the fellow was daft with drink, and, with maudlin exultation, he sprang after her and strove to seize her in his arms, laughing at her frantic blows. Then the inner door suddenly opened and tumbled them both into the hall and into the arms of a tall, dark, heavily-moustached man who looked amazed one second and enlightened the next, for he seated the half-fainting girl in a chair, kicked the intruder into the gutter, and then sprang back into the hall in time to catch her as she was almost toppling over on the tiled floor. This brought her the second time within the clasp of a muscular arm, and then she gasped an inquiry for her friends, and he sent the staring hall-boy to ask if they were in, and stepped into his own room and brought forth a glass of wine, which he calmly ordered her to sip, and then, seeing her heart was fluttering like a terrified bird's, he spoke gently and soothingly, and little by little she had regained some composure when the boy came down from the fourth floor to say the ladies were out.

Then she would have gone, and she strove to go, but her knees shook, and he sent the boy with a message and made her wait, seated in the hall chair, and came forth again from his room in a fur overcoat and cap, and a moment later a cab was at the door. She recoiled and said she could go in a car; but the cars were two blocks away. "Kindly permit me to see you safely home," he said. "You have had a terrible fright, and are in no condition to walk." At all events, she was in no condition to rebel, and was glad to sink back into the cushioned corner of the hansom. "I'll have to trouble you for the street and number," said he, apologetically, as he stepped calmly in beside her.

"Oh, indeed I mustn't trouble you to come. The driver can----" And then, alas! she remembered that she had but ten cents about her.

"The driver can, perhaps, but in this case he won't," was the grave, half-smiling answer. "Number what? Which street, if you please?"

Helplessly she gave them. Commandingly he repeated them to cabby peeping down through his pygmy man-trap in the roof, and away went the two-wheeler. Her home was but six blocks distant. "You must let me pay the cabman," she faltered, not well knowing how she was going to do so.

"I would, if it would comfort you," said he, calmly, "but he's already engaged to me by the hour for the evening."

"Then my share of it, at least," she persisted.

"That I estimate to be possibly fifteen cents," said he, as the vehicle drew up at the curb; "and I think I owe you ten times the amount for the pleasure of kicking such an arrant cur as that specimen. Has he ever annoyed you before? Do you know him?"

"By sight only," said she, the color at last reappearing in her face. "He is often on that street corner below the Beaulieu, but I do not know his name."

"He will be there less frequently in future. And now is there nothing I can do? Are you sure you have everything you need at home?"

"More than I need,"--very much more, she could have added to herself, thinking of her many unbidden lodgers,--"but you haven't given me your name, and I owe you so much--besides the fifteen cents." She was trying to smile now.

"You owe me nothing, unless----" he was turning away, but something in her sweet, earnest face drew him back,--"unless it be permission to call and ask how you are after all this excitement."

Miss Wallen's face clouded. Where could she receive him? Were not every nook and corner of the house except her own little room given over to the use of occupants in whom this distinguished-looking gentleman could be expected to feel no interest whatever? He saw the hesitation, and spoke at once.

"I beg your pardon," said he, frankly and heartily. "I had no right whatever to be intrusive. Good-night, and--better luck next time." With that he was into the cab and off in a trice.

Two days afterwards Miss Wallen called at the Beaulieu on her way down town, clambered to the fourth floor, and asked her friends the name of the gentle-man who occupied the left front room, ground-floor. They said he was a Mr. For-rest, but he'd gone away--he was often away; from which she decided him to be one of the knights errant of the commercial world, but vastly unlike in tone and manner those who usually accosted her. Two weeks afterwards, as she was seated at her desk in the big office building, while her friend Miss Bonner was clicking away at the opposite window, the door opened, and in came an elderly lawyer for whom she had done many a page of accurate work. "Miss Wallen," said he, "can you do some quick copying for a friend of mine? Let me present Lieutenant Forrest, of the regular army."

CHAPTER VI.

That Miss Wallen was no more surprised than her new customer was apparent at a glance, but there was no time wasted in remarks on previous meetings or pres-ent weather. It seemed that the gentleman in question needed three typewritten copies of a long essay he had written, and needed them at once. It was now four P.M. on Tuesday. He came for the work at five o'clock Wednesday afternoon, and, although she had wrought hard and faithfully, it lacked completion by just a page. "It will be ready in ten minutes, sir, if you can wait," said Miss Wallen, rising.

"Pray be in no hurry," said Mr. Forrest. "I have nothing to do to-night but read it over." He took a vacant chair and produced the evening paper, but through its pages he had already glanced while at the club; over its pages he was glancing now at the slender, fragile-looking girl with those busy, flying fingers and the intent gaze in her tired eyes. He saw how wan, even sallow, she looked. The lines of care were on her forehead and already settling about the corners of the soft, sensitive mouth. He did not know that all alone she had returned to the office the previous evening and worked until midnight, then hied her homeward fast as cable-car could bear her, only, with racking nerves and aching limbs, to toss through almost sleepless hours until the pallid dawn. He did not know that in order that he might have this work on time she had never left the building since eight A.M. that day. Silently she finished the last page, counted and arranged the sheets, shaking out the intervening carbons, quickly bound each set with heavier cover, and then stood before him with her work. The pale yellow gleam of the wintry twilight was streaming through the west window, the most unbecoming and trying ever girl had to face, and she faced it unflinchingly. Forrest quickly arose.

"I fear this has been heavy work, Miss Wallen," he said, regretfully. "You must make allowance for my inexperience. I have to leave town to-morrow, and needed this before going. Mr. Langston--an old friend--brought me in to you. I--I hope you will let me pay you--all I think it worth."

"I could have got along faster if the manuscript had been a little clearer," said the girl, smiling slightly. "Some of it was hard to decipher, and the technical terms were new to me. If you will look it over and let me know how nearly correct it is, I will then make out my bill accordingly."

"There won't be any time for that," said he, "and Mr. Langston says you are never inaccurate. He tells me, furthermore, that you brought my scrawl to him three times to-day for words he himself could hardly make out. It is over eighteen thousand words, according to my count. I know what such work is worth in New York,"--and now he held forth three crisp ten-dollar bills,--"but this had to be done so rapidly. Will thirty dollars be--anywhere near right?" he asked.

Miss Wallen consulted a memorandum on her desk, gravely searched through her portemonnaie, found some small coin and a two-dollar bill, then as gravely took two of the bills and handed him the ten, the two, and the small change. "More than sufficient by just twelve dollars and fifteen cents," she quietly said, "provided it be understood that you are to send me a memorandum of any and all errors detected, and I shall be here early to-morrow morning and will be glad to rewrite the pages in which they occur."

But Forrest protested. "I gave twenty-five dollars in New York for work much shorter and done leisurely," said he, "and you have worked long hours. I feel under very great obligation."

"You needn't," said she. "I have made more in the last twenty-four hours than in the previous week. I was only too glad to get the work."

Down the iron stairs clerks and office-boys were clattering. From the crowded pavement a hundred feet below, the thunder of hoofs and wheels and thronging traffic rose on the frosty air. Over the roofs, wind-driven, came the screech of a hundred whistles from foundry, factory, and mill on the wide-spreading west side. Toil-worn men by thousands were laying down their tools and turning eagerly, wearily homeward. The gongs of the cable-cars hammered mad alarums, and swarms of people squeezed upon the platforms. In adjacent office blocks the electric lights were beginning to gleam, and the pallid hues of dying day were fading from the wintry sky. Forrest's business was done, and he had no excuse to linger. She stood there facing him, evidently expecting him to go. Never before in his life had he encountered anything of this description. He had read and heard that many a girl delicately reared was now employed as book-keeper, typewriter, and stenographer, in offices all over the land, and here was one, plainly--even poorly--clad, yet proud, independent, self-reliant, and in every word and look and act, no matter how humble her lot, as unmistakably a "lady" as his own sister. He wanted to stay, wanted to impress upon her his appreciation of the service she had done him, wanted to persuade her to accept what he felt she sorely needed,--the remaining ten dollars of the sum Langston had told him would be about what she would probably charge,--but, after a moment's irresolute pause, he turned abruptly and went to the door.

"I shall be back in a month with more such work, and I shall be fortunate if I can get you to do it for me. Good-night, Miss Wallen, and--thank you."

"Good-night, sir, and thank you."

Forrest went discontentedly over to the Union League. He felt somehow that he hadn't treated that girl right. One or two men from the fort were there,--Waring of the light battery and little "Chip" Sanders of the cavalry. These jovial captains hailed him and besought him in cordial soldier fashion to stay and dine, especially in view of the long trip ahead of him on the morrow, but he begged off. He had an evening's work ahead, and must get home betimes, said he. He compromised, however, on a modest tipple, and, not caring to fight his way through the crowd in either car or street, summoned a cab and was soon comfortably trundling to the north side. One block beyond the river, under the electric lights, he caught sight of a slender, girlish form, swiftly threading a way along the pavement, and recognized at a glance the heroine of the adventure of a fortnight gone, the transcriber of those fruitful pages on the seat by his side, and the object of his thoughts.

"Hold up under those lights yonder," he cried to cabby through the trap in the roof, and cabby, seeing no bar in close proximity, marvelled as he obeyed. Forrest sprang out, turned back, and in another moment was raising his hat to the girl, who glanced up with nervous start and repellent mien that only slowly changed to recognition. Even then there was womanly reserve, and much of it, in her manner.

"Pardon me, Miss Wallen, I never dreamed of such a thing as your walking all the way home, and after such a long day's work. My cab is right here; please let me drive you the rest of the way."

"Thank you, no," she answered, quietly. "I always walk after a long day's work. It is exercise and pleasure both."

"But surely you are very late, and--forgive my reminding you of your recent unpleasant experience."

"No one else ever chased me," she said, "and I don't think even he would had he not been drinking. You seem to have scared him away, for not once have I set eyes on him since."

"But you will ride, won't you? It would be a pleasure--some comfort to my conscience--if I might send you home, after the lot that you have done and the little you would take." They had reached the cab now, and he stopped invitingly, but she never faltered, and only turned towards him and slackened her steps sufficiently to repeat her thanks and a courteous refusal.

"Upon my word, you make me ashamed of my own laziness," said Forrest. "I used to be a good tramper on the Plains, but have been getting out of the way of it. At least I may walk a little way with you, may I not?"

And this she could not well see how to decline. Cabby was dismissed with a *douceur*, and Forrest hastened after his new acquaintance. She carried some bundles in her arms, and he offered to take them. He had his own, however, and she declined. He shifted his packet of triplicates under the right arm and tendered her, with courteous bow, the left, and she "preferred to trudge along without it, thank you," yet in so pleasant a way he could not find fault. He walked all the way to her little home, and bade her good-night with the promise that when he returned in February he would be glad to have another eighteen thousand words transcribed in triplicate for seventeen dollars and odd cents.

"You can't," said she, with her same quiet smile. "It will cost eighteen at least. Your fifteen cents change to-day was for my share of the cab."

He was on duty in the judge-advocate's office of the department, as has been said, and had been ordered off on a court-martial. He was back in two weeks, and more work went through that typewriter, and then came days which he spent in study at the Lambert Library, and pages of memoranda and notes which he read to her at her office, which were faithfully stenographed and promptly, accurately typewritten, and there were soon some evening walks home,--several of them,-- and Forrest found the way curiously short as compared with the original estimate. He was deeply interested in his work at head-quarters, but the detail was only to last a month or two longer, for then the regular incumbent would have returned from the long leave of absence granted him on account of ill health, and then Forrest himself purposed spending some months abroad, all arrangements for his leave having been already consummated.

One afternoon at the library Mr. Wells came and seated himself by the lieutenant's side. They had had many a long chat together, and were fast friends.

"I'm out of luck," said Wells. "I've seen it coming for months, and ought to have been prepared. My typewriter has given me warning."

"Going to be married, I suppose?"

"Yes, and within six weeks. She's a girl I simply can't replace."

"Why not?"

"Because in my work only a well-educated and highly intelligent girl will answer. I have to dictate sometimes fifty letters a day filled with strange names and technicalities and foreignisms, and there's no time to consult dictionaries and the like,--no leisure, half the time, to read over the letters submitted for my signature. I must trust to my typewriter; and girls educated up to that standard come too high for our salary. I gradually taught Miss Stockton what she knows, so she was content with sixty dollars a month, but I can't get one who can do as well for a hundred, which is more by forty than the directors will allow me."

Forrest was silent a moment. "It is work that demands all a girl's time, I suppose?" he ventured.

"Yes, every bit of it from nine to five, and often to six. She has her evenings at home, however, unless some of our library assistants are sick; then she would have to help at the shelves."

"If you are in no great hurry, will you hold the offer open one week? I know a g--a lady, I should say, who is intelligence and accuracy combined, and who might take it. She has done much work for me, and I know her worth."

"Would she come for sixty dollars, do you suppose?"

"I will ask her," said Forrest, guardedly. He well knew how glad his hard-working typewriter would be to have so permanent and pleasant a station. He more than suspected that many men who came to the busy office in the heart of the city were far from respectful. He remembered how his blood boiled one afternoon when he found a bulky fellow, his hat on the back of his head, his legs outstretched, and a vile cigar tiptilted in his mouth, sitting leering beside her desk.

"You shouldn't permit it," he said to her, later.

"Ah, but I must not quarrel with my bread and butter," was her reply, half mournful, half whimsical. "Not one man in ten thinks of taking off his hat or dropping his cigar when he enters our 'shop.' No, Mr. Forrest, we are wage-workers who can't afford to draw the line at the manners of our customers."

"But--are there not some who--who become impertinent--familiar--if not checked at the start?" he found himself constrained to ask, and the flame that shot into her cheeks told him his suspicion was correct.

"Not often," she answered, presently, "and never more than once. We simply try not to notice small impertinences, Miss Bonner and I, and generally, you know, we are together here."

This was mid-April. The vacancy was to occur at the end of the month. Forrest himself brought Miss Wallen to the library and presented her to Mr. Wells. A gentleman was seated in the librarian's room at the time,--an industrious fellow who had recently appeared, who spent some hours turning over many books, and whom Wells described as a most interesting and travelled man, a graduate of Jena, etc.; but at sight of him Miss Wallen showed slight though unmistakable signs of embarrassment, almost annoyance. He pretended to busy himself with his books, but was evidently listening to what was going on, and Miss Wallen was decidedly constrained. Presently he arose and came forward, saying, with much suavity of manner, "You must pardon my intrusion. I could not but catch something of this conversation, and had I known before that Mr. Wells was contemplating a change here I should have eagerly availed myself of the privilege our friendship gives to recommend this young lady, of whose character and qualifications--we being inmates of the same household--I can speak *ex cathedra*, as it were, and can hardly speak too highly." He went on to say more, taking the floor, as was his custom, to the exclusion of everybody else, and Mr. Forrest withdrew to a distant part of the room. Miss Wallen presently bade Mr. Wells good-night and asked when she might come to see him again, and Wells, looking a trifle vexed, asked for her address and said he would write.

And then Mr. Elmendorf announced that it would give him much pleasure to see Miss Wallen home, and what could she do? Forrest had said nothing about going further. Elmendorf had certainly been most flattering in his commendation. She had taken a decided dislike to him during the few weeks he had occupied the lodger's room, and had avoided him as much as possible, but it might well be that he was a man of influence in library matters. She had no reason for rebuffing, but good reason for showing gratitude. Forrest gravely bade her good-evening and good luck, and Miss Wallen walked away with her lodger in close attendance. All the way home he descanted on his influence with Wells and the trustees. He was already, he said, contemplating taking a position in the household of Mr. Allison, the millionaire magnate. He took it, in truth, within the week, and wrote Miss Wallen that it had given him much pleasure to urge warmly her claim for the position soon to become vacant. He found they had several other applications, and some who had strong influence, but he would not cease to urge her appointment and keep her well-being in mind. But meantime one day Mr. Wells gladdened the girl's heart by a brief note saying that he had been so favorably impressed with the work she had done for Mr. Forrest that he had determined to tender her the place.

Two days later Forrest came to congratulate her and to bid her adieu, as he would sail for Europe within the week. She tried to thank him, but could not frame the words. She did not lack for language, however, when her mother read to her that night the charming note she had just received from Mr. Elmendorf, felicitating her upon the promotion of her devoted and dutiful daughter, and himself upon the fact that this good fortune was probably due to his determined and persistent presentation of her daughter's claims before the trustees, whom he had frequent opportunity of meeting at Mr. Allison's house. Doubtless Elmendorf considered this presentation equivalent in full for the three weeks' arrears of room rent, a cheque for which he had said should be forthcoming as soon as Mr. Allison paid in advance his first quarter's salary, but which never came at all.

CHAPTER VII.

When Mr. Forrest returned from Europe in the late autumn of '93, he expected to go forthwith to the station of his regiment and devote his energies to those ceaseless, engrossing, yet somewhat narrowing duties that keep a man of mature years, capable of much better things, attending roll-calls, drilling two sets of fours addressed by courtesy as "company," grilling on the rifle-range, and consuming hours of valuable time in work allotted in older services to sergeants. Calling at the War Department on his way, he was asked about the autumn manoeuvres and if he had seen any of them. He had seen a great deal, the interest of friends in both the German and Austrian services having enabled him to follow the armies assembled about Metz and Guens to excellent advantage. Returning to his billet after each long day in the saddle, he had spent some hours before retiring in recording his impressions and observations, the result being several big note-books crammed with data of deep interest to the professional soldier. The adjutant-general took Forrest in to the Secretary of War, and there was some significant talk, the result of which was the intimation that he should again be assigned to temporary duty at department head-quarters in Chicago in order to give him opportunity to write out his notes. Long before this, Forrest's essays on grand tactics and certain papers on military history had won much favor among the studious men in the army, and it was with pride and pleasure that he entered on the allotted task. He wrote, as did Zachary Taylor, a hand that looked much as though a ramrod rather than a pen had been used, and naturally his first thought was to find his transcriber of the previous winter. There she was at her desk in the library, and looking far younger, happier, and better than when he saw her last, and the frank pleasure in her face was good to see as she welcomed him more in manner than in words.

"Certainly," said Miss Wallen; "I shall be glad to give as many evenings to the work as may be necessary. I am too busy here by day." And so as the autumn wore out and the winter wore on, her slender white fingers danced over the keys, and page after page, in neatly typed duplicates, his voluminous notes on the armies of

Germany and Austria-Hungary were faithfully transcribed. Home was not so far away now, and her brisk walks led her no longer through sections she had learned to dread. Accustomed for some years to far longer and lonelier tramps in the wintry evenings, she thought nothing of tripping to and fro between the Lambert and the rather crowded little house in which she dwelt. Mart and his wife and babies still sojourned there, and the babies waxed strong and loud and lusty on Aunt Jenny's bounty, never caring whose fingers earned the porridge, so long as their share was ample and frequent. Mart was out of work, and correspondingly out of elbows and temper. Mart had taken to continual meetings and to such drink as he could get treated to or credit for, and still the mother condoned, the wife complained, and Jenny carried the family load. Mart loved to tread the rostrum boards and portray himself as a typical victim of corporation perfidy and capitalistic greed. The railway company from which he had seceded refused to take him back, and other companies, edified by the reports of his speeches in *The Switch Light*, *The Danger Signal*, and other publications avowedly devoted to the interest of the down-trodden operatives of the railway and manufacturing companies, thought that in a winter when many poor fellows were out of work through no fault of their own, beyond having exercised the right of suffrage the wrong way, the few vacancies should be given to men more likely to render faithful service. Mart's wife, impressed with the idea that she must do something, took in sewing, and took the sewing to ask Jenny to show her how, which in nine cases out of ten Jenny did practically. If the little money thus earned had gone to pay for the babies' milk or Mart's whiskey bills, Jenny would have been grateful; but even these shillings, earned with her numbed and weary fingers, somehow found their way to Mart's broad palm and thence to the dram-shop, though not to that which had claims for goods already delivered. And then followed scenes that covered the poor girl with shame and indignation. To her office at the library one winter evening, when Wells was reading the late mail, and Mr. Forrest, seated at a neighboring desk with a big atlas before him was far away among the glinting *pickelhaubes* on the banks of the Moselle, a man came with an account which he wished Miss Wallen to settle. It was Martin Wallen's bar bill for the autumn months at Donnelly's Shades, and the girl flushed with mortification. "This is something with which I have nothing to do," said she. "I would not pay it if I had the money."

"I was told to come to you," said the man. "It's your brother's account, and he said you'd promised him the money time and again. If it ain't paid we'll send for the furniture." And then he wanted to show it to Wells, who waved him off in annoyance; and then he looked as though he would like to interest the other occupant of the room in the matter, but something about that gentleman's face as he arose and came forward proved unsympathetic. "I'll send this bill in again on the 31st," said Mr. Donnelly, "and if it ain't paid then----"

But the tall, brown-eyed, brown-moustached man was walking straight at him, looking him through and through, and there would have been a collision in the office had not Donnelly backed promptly out through the door-way. This merely transferred the scene of it and involved a third party, for there, just outside the ground-glass partition, ostensibly hunting for a book in the revolving case and humming a lively tune, was Elmendorf. Recoiling to avoid contact with the advancing Forrest, the bill-collector backed into the listening tutor and bumped him up against a table.

"Oh, beg pardon," said Elmendorf, as though in no wise aware who his bumper might be, and then edged off towards the corridor beyond, apparently desirous of escaping further connection with the affair. But Forrest, even in the dim light of the anteroom, recognized him at a glance. More and more, ever since the return from Europe, had he grown to dislike and distrust the man. More than once had he seen an expression on Miss Wallen's face when Wells happened to mention Elmendorf that gave ground for the belief that she, too, had no pleasant recollection of her erstwhile lodger; but never had she opened her lips upon the subject. Indeed, bright and intelligent as was the girl when she chose to talk, both Wells and Forrest had found that when she preferred to be silent it was useless to question. But here, skulking in the anteroom, where reading was out of the question, where, however, one might easily hear what was going on in the private office, here was Elmendorf again, and though Donnelly's foot-falls were audible to all as he came pounding up the stairway and turned from the corridor into the office rooms, not a sound of others had been heard. The main stairway--that which led to the great reading-rooms of the library proper--was on the southern front. Only those having business with the head librarian or the trustees were supposed to come this way. Forrest often read, wrote, and studied here, because the more valuable atlases and books of reference were near at hand, and whenever not writing for Wells Miss Wallen was at work on his notes. It flashed upon Forrest that the tutor had some object other than book-hunting in that noiseless visit, and he called him back. "Would you mind waiting a moment, Mr. Elmendorf?" said he. "I should like to speak with you after I've said a word to this--gentleman." Then, coolly pushing beyond both, he closed the corridor door and turned on the electric light.

"Mr. Donnelly," said he, facing the now nervous-looking Irishman, "you know as well as I that no woman on earth is liable for the liquor bills of any man, even a relative. What brought you here?"

"Me legs, I s'pose, an' me own affairs. What's it to you, anyhow?" But Donnelly was shifting rather unsteadily on those same legs and twisting his bill in his hands.

"This, to begin with," said Forrest, very coolly, though his blood was boiling, and the impulse to floor the fellow was strong within him. "An old fellow campaigner of mine, Sergeant McGrath, has told me----" but there was no need to go further. Donnelly's tone and manner underwent instant change.

"Is this Lieutenant Forrest?"

"It is Lieutenant Forrest; and I have this to say to you here and now. You came here to bring shame and distress on an honest girl,--you, an old soldier and an Irishman,--the first soldier and the first Irishman I ever knew to be guilty of so low and contemptible a piece of persecution. When I write to Major Cranston of this, and when I tell McGrath----"

"Don't be hard on me, lieutenant. I meant no harm to the lady at all. Sure the bill's been unpaid ever since October. I tuk it to the house--I thought mebbe she could inflooence Mart, but I'd never have come here wid it at all, sorr, but--but----" And his troubled gaze wandered now to where Elmendorf stood biting his nails and watching a chance to speak.

"But what, Donnelly? Who put you up to such a dirty piece of business?"

"Permit me. Nothing dirty was intended for a minute, if I may be allowed to speak," said Elmendorf, as he came forward. "As a friend of all parties concerned, for I know Mr. Wallen well and have remarked his bibulous propensities with distress, I merely suggested to Mr. Donnelly that perhaps if he could get Miss Wallen's ear he might possibly induce her to exercise a restraining influence upon her brother. I thought it best that she should know how and where he was spending so much money *in esse* as well as money *in posse*. That Mr. Donnelly should have misconstrued my well-meant words into----"

"Oh, sure ye told me to show this bill when everybody could see it, sorr, and that would take the starch out av her."

"Settle it between you, gentlemen," said Mr. Forrest, turning contemptuously away. "I have heard more than enough."

"I will see you about this later this evening," said Elmendorf, as the lieutenant disappeared within the sanctum, slamming the door after him and vouchsafing no answer.

That evening Wells's letters seemed interminable. It was nearly half-past six when he finished dictating, and with aching heart and burning face Miss Wallen closed her desk and silently went for her cloak and overshoes. For over half an hour Mr. Forrest had stood to his guns across the room, making much pretence of being busy with the atlas and his notes, but time and again his eyes wandered, following his thoughts, to the other two,--Wells rapidly dictating, his stenographer with bowed head, determinedly wielding her pencil. When Wells finally started, the lieutenant arose and strolled out with him, closing the door behind them. "I shall see Miss Wallen home," said he, in low tone. "She's had more than enough indignity for one day."

"I'd do it if you couldn't, Mr. Forrest, even though they're waiting for me at home. That girl's a lady, by Jupiter! You've no idea how she's studied and developed ever since she's been here; and it's a damned outrage that such fellows should be allowed to annoy her."

"Such fellows won't, another time," said Forrest, quietly. "Elmendorf was back of this, for some reason that I mean to fathom."

"That's all very well as far as the Irishman's concerned, Mr. Forrest,--he's had his fill,--but look out for that other. I'm no judge of character, now, if he isn't a snake."

When Forrest re-entered the room Miss Wallen had turned out the electric lights over her desk and was standing by the window, her face bowed in her thin white hands. Forrest's overcoat and hat always hung in the closet without. He had gone with Wells, closing the door. She was, as she supposed, at last alone, and the reaction had come. All the weary months of work, work, work, all the patient slaving to provide for the improvident, all the brave, cheery, hopeful, uncomplaining days of honest toil and honest effort, only to end in such a scene of shame and mortification as this! What could Mr. Wells think of his secretary, chased to her desk with the liquor-bills of her kindred! What would not Mr. Forrest think! A weaker woman would have found refuge and comfort in a passion of tears, but her eyes seemed burning. Leaning against the open casement, she stood there fairly quivering with wrath and the sense of indignity and wrong. She, too, had recognized Elmendorf's nasal whine in the anteroom, and felt well assured that he was in some way responsible for Donnelly's action. Mart had had much to say of late of the foreigner's convincing logic and thrillingly eloquent appeals to the working-man. *There* was the man to wring the neck of capital and bring the bloated bond-holders to terms, said he. Mart never missed a meeting where Elmendorf was to speak, and had more than once been brought home, fuddled, in the cab which conveyed the agitator back to the scene of his labors in the Allison homestead. The cab was paid for by the Union, and Elmendorf didn't mind having it wait outside while he assisted Mart within and stopped to condole with Mrs. Wallen the elder, or Mrs. Wallen junior, and to inquire significantly, if he did not see her, where Miss Wallen was; he always supposed the library closed at nine o'clock, and was not aware, he said, that anybody except the janitor was permitted to remain there later. He knew very well that the librarian was sometimes there until nearly midnight. He knew well that it was there and in the evenings, mainly, that Miss Wallen worked at the transcript of Forrest's reports. "At least," as he said to himself, and suggested to others, "that is the *ostensible* purpose of her frequently prolonged visits." He often walked by the lighted windows of the sanctum and occasionally slipped into the dark hall-way, so the watchman later said. The same irrepressible propensity to meddle in the affairs of everybody in the household where he was employed, in the councils of the various labor unions, in the meetings of political associations, in the official duties or off-hand chats of the men at military head-quarters, in the management of the Lambert Library, seemed to follow him in his casual intercourse with this obscure little household. One night when towards ten o'clock Miss Wallen came blithely down the corridor stairs, she was surprised to find the tutor awaiting her. "As I know Mr. Forrest to be otherwise engaged to-night, Miss Wallen, I have ventured to offer my services as escort," said he, and though she shrank from and could not bear him, there was no reason at that time for denying him; but when he presently began talking of Forrest in his suggestive, insinuating way, and excusing his references to the lieutenant on the ground of his extreme regard for her widowed mother, her impoverished but amiable relatives, and her own refined, intellectual, and accomplished self, she shrank still more and strove to silence him,--a difficult matter. She had, however, a trait that proved simply exasperating to a man of Elmendorf's calibre,--a faculty of listening in absolute silence where she did not desire to confirm or approve,--and when he had spent much breath and nearly half an hour in descanting upon his impressions of the demoralizing tendencies of military associations in general and of idle officers in particular, it rasped him to find that she did not seem to consider his views worthy the faintest comment; nor would she nor did she invite him in. When her mother reproved her for this, Miss Wallen smiled, and said, "Next time I will, and then you might ask him for the three weeks' lodging he hasn't paid," and Mart said she ought to be ashamed of speaking so of a man who had done everything for her. She'd never have got that library place at all if it hadn't been for Elmendorf, no matter what her fine friends might have told her. Oh, Mart knew all about it; needn't try to pull the wool over his eyes! Another time had Elmendorf come, and again had he talked more of what he had done for her and the rights it gave him to tender her counsel, and this time his references to Forrest took a graver form and became offensive. It was then, indignant, she refused to hear more of it, and that night Elmendorf went away gritting his teeth, and now had come this contemptible essay to humiliate her before her employer. Oh, it was cowardly! shameful! She threw up her arms, clinching her little white hands and stamping as slender a foot as ever walked in a machine-made shoe, and then, ejaculating, as women will, in moments of supreme exasperation, "If I were only a man!" whirled about and beheld one.

"In your present mood," said Mr. Forrest, quietly, "I am rather glad you are not, especially as what I have to say refers to you rather in your capacity as 'the clever woman of the family.' Did you ever read an English book of that title?" And then in the most matter-of-fact way in the world he proceeded to assist her into the heavy winter cloak he had lifted from its accustomed peg. "No, of course you haven't," he went on, chatting unconcernedly, and well knowing she was too overwrought to talk at all; "a girl who works from morning till late at night has little chance to read anything beyond stenographic notes and hideous hieroglyphics--mine, for instance. Now, this sensible head-gear, if you please---- How can a woman wear a hat in winter? Yes, it's on quite straight,--quite as straight as though you had a glass in front of you. Now the overshoes. No, pardon me, Miss Wallen, you're not going to put them on yourself. Sit down, if you please, or stand, if you don't." And down he dropped on one knee and in a trice had stowed away the thin, worn little boots, with their frayed button-holes, within the warm yet clumsy Arctics. "You are sensible to wear such things as these," he said. "The snow is falling heavily, and I mean to walk you home to-night. Now the gloves.--Yes, you may have your own way there, as I shouldn't know how." And, so saying, he seemed calmly to have taken possession of the hitherto self-willed and independent young woman, who for the first time in her life began to realize how much sweetness there was, after all, in having some one to do something for one, instead of being expected to do everything for every one else. She submitted silently to be led forth into the cool, fresh evening air, and then when he as calmly took her hand and placed it within his arm she made no move to withdraw it, neither did she seem to know how by means of it to lean upon his strength. Passively she let it lie, and, walking by his side, turned her face to the drifting snowflakes and cared not that the night was raw and chill, the lake wind blustering.

For a moment more Forrest did not speak. He glanced keenly up the dim avenue, holding his head very high, as was his way, and himself very erect. Already the sting and shame of her recent experience seemed fading in Jenny's past. There was something so new, strange, sweet, in this masterful assumption on his part of all control and command, there was something so complete in her faith in him, something so like girlish admiration if not hero-worship surging up in the throbbing little heart beneath that worn old winter cloak, that much of her old bright, buoyant, merry self came back to her. "If I can't be a man," said she to herself, "I'm the next thing to one, if there ever was one," and then was amazed at her own impulse to peer up into his grave, soldierly face and aghast to find herself drawing closer to his side. In the suddenness and alarm of this revelation she nearly jumped beyond arm's length, and he felt constrained to retake her hand and draw it farther through his arm.

"You will find it easier if you will let me bear a little of the weight to-night," said he, gravely, "and that is why I have made it my business to intrude upon your time and attention. Miss Wallen, will you kindly tell me what claim your brother has upon you?"

"He *is* my brother and out of work," she answered, simply.

"Can't he get work?"

"He says he can't."

"What can he do?"

"He writes well, and he had a clerkship, but Mart was--unsteady, and he lost it. Then he got a place in the freight-yards, but there was a strike, and he went out. They wouldn't take him back then because he was so foolish in his talk; and they can't take him now, for hundreds of better men, steadier men, old employees, have been laid off. Ever since the World's Fair business has been falling away."

"And you have had not only that house and your mother to care for, but an able-bodied brother?"

Jenny dropped her head. Able-bodied brother, indeed!--with wife, babies, debts, duns, and all! She had borne the weight of the whole establishment upon her fragile shoulders; but that wasn't a thing to speak of to him,--to anybody. Her silence touched him.

"Do you mean that out of your little salary you have paid that house-rent and all the expenses and your mother's and his too?"

No answer.

"I wish you would tell me," he said, in such grave, courteous tones that they went to her heart. "I beg you not to think me intrusive. I have never heard of such a case before. Why, Miss Wallen, I'm appalled when I see how thoughtless I have been. You simply cannot afford the time to work for me at the price you fixed."

"It pays better than mending Mart's clothes, etc., at home," said she, whimsically; "very much better than anything I can get to do up town."

"Good heavens! cannot your mother mend Mart's clothes? Can't he mend them himself? My--my--poor little friend, I had no idea matters were as bad as this!"

He had no idea even now how bad matters were, nor did she care to edify him. "Why, Mr. Forrest," said she, "when I look around me this winter and see all the want and suffering on every side--the absolute destitution in places--I think my fortune regal. I only wish all the girls I know of were half as well-to-do."

Forrest drew a long breath. "Well, of all the incarnations of pluck and cheerfulness I ever heard of, commend me to this," thought he. They were within two squares of home, and at the corner was a large family grocery store. She faltered now. "I'm very much obliged to you for coming with me so far, and--I have to stop here."

"But only to make some purchases. You are going on to tea, and I have something I want to say."

"I may have to wait, and you have your engagements."

"Nothing in the world but to dine, *solus*, at the Virginia, and my appetite's about gone. I mean to wait, Miss Wallen."

Miss Wallen flushed, but made no further remonstrance. Entering the store, she gave her orders. Some little packages of tea and sugar were speedily ready. In the window were some pyramids of Florida oranges, rich and luscious fruit. Watching her with uncontrollable interest, he saw her eyes glancing towards them, saw and knew the question framed by her soft lips, saw and realized what was passing as the salesman answered and she shook her head. Turning to another clerk, he pencilled a number on a card he handed him and gave some orders of his own. Presently she stored her change in the little portemonnaie and picked up her bundles. Promptly he relieved her of them, and again as they came forth he tendered his arm. The side street into which they turned was darker than the broad avenue. The houses were poor and cheap, the gas-lamps few and far between. Silently now they walked rapidly along, for he was deep in thought. He longed to find some way of opening the subject uppermost in his mind, but knew not how. At last he spoke:

"Miss Wallen, where and how can I see your brother? I've an idea of a place he might fill. He is unmarried, I presume?"

Silence a moment. "No, Mart has a wife."

"A wife? Where is she? What does she do?"

"She isn't strong, and can't do much of anything."

"Not even mend his clothes, or stop---- How about children?"

"You know the old adage," said she, with a quiet smile, "and Mart is a poor man."

"And they, too, are your care--you their support--and--this has been going on since last year?"

"Oh, no; Mart gets odd jobs now and then."

"The proceeds of which he spends in---- But I entreat your pardon, my--my friend. This is beyond anything I ever dreamed of; and--don't come to the library to-night, please. There's no hurry about those pages; to-morrow night will be better."

They were at the little gateway now, and he released her arm. Over-against them on the opposite side of the street two men, skulking back in the shadows of a dark entrance-way, edged a little farther forward, watched him as he restored the bundles, watched him as he took again her hand, then lifted his hat and bowed over it as he might have done reverence to a queen, watched her as she tripped within-doors, and then Forrest again as he slowly turned and walked thoughtfully away.

"That's the man, then?" asked, in cautious, querulous tone, the shorter, slighter of the two.

"That's him--damn him! I can feel his kick to this day."

"And it was with him--in his room--she took refuge? you could swear to it?"

"'Course I could, on a stack of Bibles."

And this was early in the week of Mr. Elmendorf's conversation with Aunt Lawrence, only forty-eight hours prior to the sudden orders which prevented Mr. Forrest's dining at the Allisons' and escorting Miss Florence to the opera, and which hurried him miles away on a mission whereof only two other men at head-quarters knew the purport,--the general and his chief of staff. There was good reason for the aides-de-camp an "understrappers," as Elmendorf referred to them, being even more mysterious than usual.

CHAPTER VIII.

There was a month or more during the late winter in which Mr. Elmendorf, cold-shouldered out of official society at department head-quarters, became quite the managing director of the Allison mansion. John Allison, with a party of fellow-magnates, was on a long tour of inspection over the southernmost of the transcontinental lines, and, finding home life a trifle uncongenial just now, owing to some discussions with Aunt Lawrence, finding, too, that the wives and daughters of other

magnates were to accompany them on the trip, sojourning days at a time in many
of the charming resorts among the mountains or along the Pacific seaboard, Miss
Allison eagerly accepted their invitation to be one of the party. Mrs. Lawrence was
to remain in charge at home, and was permitted to send for and receive under her
wing her own graceless duckling, with the distinct understanding that he was in no
wise to be allowed to interfere with Cary's studies or duties. Allison "had no use,"
as he expressed it, for his nephew Lawrence. He had helped pull the cub through
many a scrape, but had tired of it, and having secured him a place in an Eastern office where he had enough to live on and little to do, desired to wash his hands of
him in future; but mother-love watches over even the renegades from the home
circle, and Mrs. Lawrence persuaded Brother John that Herbert's health was failing
and that he sorely needed change and rest and coddling. The brother growled out
something cynical about Chicago as a winter resort, but told her to go ahead. The
party left in early February, and about the last thing before going Allison had another conference with Elmendorf. The latter had received warning that, unless he
gave more time to the instruction of his pupil and less to that of the populace, the
engagement would terminate. Elmendorf argued, and Allison cut him short. "I have
listened to this for over eight months, and am further from conviction than ever,
Mr. Elmendorf," said he. "So waste no more eloquence on me. Take your choice between serving me on salary or writing 'screamers' and speeches for nothing. You've
done no great harm outside as yet, but there is a growing tendency to disorder that
such counsels as yours will only serve to stimulate." A blunt man was Allison, and
furnished excellent text for Elmendorf's article on The Brutality of Capital, which
presently appeared, but over a very different *nom de plume*, in the columns of the
socialistic press. Elmendorf agreed that of course, as his employer took such extreme views of the case, he must perforce acquiesce in the decision. He agreed not
to appear on the platform or write any more leaders so long as he should remain in
John Allison's employ, and then, when Allison was well beyond range, interpreted
the agreement to suit himself.

As a means of increasing his influence over the mother, Elmendorf made himself useful and agreeable to young Lawrence when he came. The lessons went on
with fair regularity, Cary and his tutor occupying their study each day until luncheon-time, and again, occasionally, later in the afternoon or evening. But, while

he no longer appeared on the stage or rostrum as one of the leading speakers of the evening, the eloquent gentleman was pretty sure to be heard from the body of the house or the midst of the audience at the various meetings held from time to time in what were referred to as "the disturbed districts." There was a familiar ring about many of the articles that appeared in the papers, but they were no longer fulminated over his name or initials. For several weeks no more dinner-parties were given at the Allisons', and few officers called there. Then the general commanding went off on a tour of inspection, taking a brace of aides with him, and these were Forrest's friends and associates and the men who least liked the tutor. But while Elmendorf had ceased to spend some time each afternoon in the offices adjoining the general's sanctum, picking up all stray items of military news and haranguing such men as would listen, his was by no means an unfamiliar figure about the great building. True to his policy, he had made acquaintance among the clerks, messengers, etc., first appearing among them as an associate and friend of their superior officers, thereby commanding, as it were, their respectful attention, and then, after studying their personal characteristics, little by little establishing confidential relations. Simple-minded, straightforward fellows, as a rule, were these soldier clerks, men who lived in a groove and knew little of the wiles of the outer world. A few there were of the decayed gentleman stamp, and other few of the bibulous. Through their hands passed much of the correspondence, in their keeping were many of the secrets, of the official life of the far-spreading department, and Elmendorf saw his opportunity. It was no difficult matter to assert in his confidential chats, conducted only when and where their superiors could get no wind of them, that he had been told by his friend the adjutant-general or by Captain and Aide-de-Camp So-and-so all about the matter in question, and all he asked was some little item of corroborative detail. Now, there were days, as the winter wore away, when sundry things had happened within the limits of the general's command which the news-gatherers of the Chicago press, always sensational, were eager to exploit, not so much, perhaps, as they actually occurred, but as the management and direction of each paper desired to make it appear they had. The reporters sounded many a possible source of information without avail, for the chief of staff had cautioned his clerks and subordinates. Great were his surprise and disgust, therefore, to find the columns suddenly blossoming out with glowing particulars of matters he had supposed discreetly hidden. The reports were by no means truthful,--they were even more than customarily colored and exaggerated,--but there was the foundation of fact in more than one. Next it began to be noted that Elmendorf, hitherto a contributor only to papers of the socialistic stamp, was frequently to be seen hobnobbing with the reporters of the prominent journals. Now, these gentlemen, as a rule, are shrewd judges of human nature and quick to determine between the gold and the glitter, between the actual possessor of important news and the mere pretender; but there was another period of a month or six weeks in which Elmendorf was sought and followed almost as eagerly as the adjutant-general himself. Never, perhaps, in his varied life had the graduate of Jena rolled in sweeter clover than during the months of the late winter and early spring of '94. An oracle at the table in a luxurious home, with no one to dispute his sway and no one actually to disapprove, unless it were his much disgusted but helpless pupil, with access to public offices and public libraries, with occasional touch with officials who might and did dislike but could not actually snub him, with occasional driblets of information to supply foundation and a vivid imagination to do the rest, he found himself an object of interest to the men of all others whom he most desired to influence,--the reporters of the daily press. Elmendorf was never in higher feather. He was even able to neglect for a time the clamors of his erstwhile hearers, his suffering brethren among the sons of toil.

And he had been managing matters at home with rare diplomacy, too. Mrs. Lawrence was mad to find out just exactly what peccadillo had brought about Mr. Floyd Forrest's sudden relief from duty at Chicago and orders to proceed to the frontier; but this was a subject on which the tutor was now decidedly coy. He had given Mrs. Lawrence to understand that because of some scandal and to prevent further talk the officer had been summarily sent away. Finding that none of the officers knew what had brought about the order, he worked among the clerks,--who knew nothing at all. One of these latter lived not far from the Lambert Library, was a tippler at times, and had a grievance. Forrest had twice come upon him when he was boisterously drunk, and, recognizing him, had given him warning, Forrest was only a "casual" at head-quarters, said the clerk, and when a fellow was off duty what he did "was none of Forrest's damned business." Elmendorf found he didn't know what had brought about Forrest's relief, and so proceeded to ask him if he'd ever heard this and that,--which the man had not, but was glad to hear now. Later,

Elmendorf made him acquainted, one cold evening, at a comfortable groggery not too far from the Allison house, with a young fellow who could and did tell how he had followed a girl whom he suspected and saw her go to Forrest's lodgings. That he made no mention of certain concomitant facts, such as his being kicked into the gutter by the lieutenant and the girl's being a total stranger to that officer at that time, was due perhaps to native modesty and possibly to Elmendorf's editorial skill. What Elmendorf wanted to create at head-quarters was the belief that it was for some such indiscretion that Forrest was exiled, well reasoning that then the entire establishment would suddenly bethink itself of all manner of suspicious circumstances that it had thought nothing of before.

He planned equally well at home. Miss Allison knew only that Forrest was ordered away on duty for an indefinite time, and speedily went away herself on the jaunt to the Pacific. Mrs. Lawrence, who longed to say something to her niece upon the subject, was cautioned by Elmendorf to say nothing at all until he could place her in possession of all the facts, which he promised shortly to do. He felt somehow that if Allison ever consulted Forrest as to the propriety of further employing him, the days of tutorship and ease were ended; but Forrest was gone, with a stab in the back, and gone probably not to return. Allison's stay promised to be prolonged until mid-April, possibly May. Miss Wallen, bending over her task at the Lambert Library, mutely avoided, and Wells openly scowled at, Elmendorf whenever he sauntered into the rooms where once he was welcome. So again he took an interest in Mart and his meanderings. Mart had steadied a bit, had a job over among the lumber-yards on the north branch, and had been keeping away from the meetings on the west side; but it wasn't a fortnight before Mart was staying out late at night again and coming home without his wits or wages Sunday mornings and denouncing his employers as scoundrels and some new men as scabs. The next thing poor Jenny knew, Mart's unpaid bills were coming to her again, and the brother had lost his situation a third time. There was no extra work now to add to her earnings, no strong, manly, courteous, thoughtful fellow to help her into her cloak and out of her troubles. The days lengthened, and so did the faces at home; so would the bills have done had she ever yielded to the importunities of her Mrs.-Nickleby-like mother or Mart's weakling of a wife; but Jenny was Spartan in self-denial; what she couldn't pay for on the spot she wouldn't have.

More and more, however, she recognized in Elmendorf the evil genius of the family, and implored Mart to have no more to do with him, whereat Mart laughed wildly. "Just you wait a bit, missy," he declaimed. "The day is coming when capitalists and corporations will bow down to him as they have to the Goulds and Vanderbilts in the past. I tell you, in less than two months, if they don't come to our terms, if they refuse to listen to our dictation not one wheel will turn from one end of this country to the other. We'll tie up the business of the whole United States, by God! That's what'll happen to capital."

"And then what will happen to us, Mart,--to you, your wife and babies,--to your mother and to me? Where will the money come from?"

"Oh, there's money enough--more than enough--millions more than enough--to feed and clothe and keep us all in luxury--tied up in the coffers of those bondholders, and when the men whose hands have made it get their hands once more on it----"

"Mart, Mart, your head is crazed with whiskey," laughed Jenny, sadly. "No wonder capital is being withdrawn from us; no wonder the gold is going back to Europe. People who have it dare not invest in communities where the employees are allowed to talk as they are here. If I had a million to invest, do you think I'd venture it where the workmen openly threatened they'd stop every wheel throughout the land? You are killing your own prospects, Mart, simply to cripple theirs."

"I don't care. What do you know of such things, anyhow? I don't mean to stand by and see my brothers starving and swindled day by day down there at Pullman."

"Who have the greater claims, Mart, those whom you call your brothers down there at Pullman, or your wife and children here at home? I feel for those people just as much as you do,--more probably,--but your duty lies here."

"Oh, that's right. Stand by your swell friends, and toss it into my teeth that I and mine are sponging on you for a living, and you want your money. Make a man more desperate than he is by your nagging and fault-finding. Drive a fellow to striking one minute and then torment him with accusations the next. I tell you if it comes to riot and bloodshed here, it's--it's just women like you--that'll--that'll have brought it all about."

But this was a statement so absurd that Jenny turned away in speechless indignation. What was the use of logic or argument with one of her brother's mental make-up? Leaving Mart to go on with his harangue and confirm the mother and his wife in their view of her utter lack of appreciation of her brother's noble nature, the girl walked wearily away to her desk at the library. It was barely eight o'clock, and her duties began only at nine, but she was an early bird, this New World Little Dorrit, and loved to be promptly at her work, and the janitor and scrub-women often listened to her cheery song as she plied the duster among the shelves and desks of the sanctum. Wells, perhaps, never noticed how much neater everything looked since Miss Wallen took charge, but she was a dainty creature, in whose eyes dusty books and littered desks were abominations. Mrs. Wells, however, was not so blind.

"That girl's worth two of Miss Stockton," was the lady's verdict, and then, noting with self-comforting criticism the inexpensive material of Jenny's gown, the absence of all attempt at ornamentation, as well, alas! as of her predecessor's brilliancy of color and clearness of skin, she added conclusively, "and she isn't pretty."

And these raw blustering days of late winter and early spring--or something--had left their mark upon poor Jenny's grave and gentle face. The circles seemed purpler and deeper under the soft dark eyes. There was even less of color in the pallid skin. There was something languid, almost droopy, in her carriage now. She had fought her fight without repining or complaint all the long months through, and knew, alas! that she was only losing ground. A year agone she looked forward with joy to this position, and now she was loaded with even heavier cares and burdens. She had found some outside work, but everything she made was rapidly swallowed up by her home cormorants. "It would be just the same, perhaps, if I had five hundred dollars a month," said Jenny. She was blue, disheartened, and discouraged,--perhaps a little weak,--as she walked rapidly on. She thought a sight of the foam-crested waves might stir her sluggish blood, and so sped eastward a block or two and out upon the lake front. Passing the Allison homestead south of the Park, she saw the family carriage just rolling away,--not the open barouche that had once so nearly run her down, but the heavy, closed carriage. She knew the coachman and the handsome bays at a glance. A few blocks farther south she again turned westward to resume her way to the library, and came suddenly upon two men standing in close conversation. One was haranguing the other, speaking in nasal, querulous, unmistakable tones and the speaker's back was towards her. Overcome by a sudden sense of repulsion, she hesitated, stopped, and was about to turn back and cross the street, when the listening party glanced up, saw the girl as she halted and seemed to be watching them, and, all in an instant, turned and sneaked, or rather lurched, up the street. Miss Wallen knew that gait in an instant. There was the ruffian who had chased her and seized her that never-to-be-forgotten night.

And here, turning about now and facing her, was Elmendorf.

For an instant the tutor's *aplomb* was gone. He stammered as he raised his hat and bade her good-morning. "I was just giving some advice to a poor devil who accosted me for alms, Miss Wallen," he said, lamely, "but I seem to have driven him off. My speeches are not universally well received, as you probably know." But Jennie was in no mood for conversation. With but scant recognition, she pushed rapidly on, and Elmendorf followed.

"There is a matter I much desire to speak about," said he, placing himself at her side. "I'm aware I have not the good fortune to stand well in Miss Wallen's opinion," he added, with a half-sneer, "and a man more vindictive and less devoted to principle would have felt like resenting the--the slights you have seen fit to put upon me. I shall observe your prohibition with regard to the--alleged officer and gentleman of whom I had occasion to speak to you, since his superiors have taken that responsibility off my hands by summarily sending him away, and as it is not likely that he will ever cross your path in this neighborhood again,--a matter in which I find sincere cause for rejoicing, for of all men I have ever met he seemed to me the least worthy of such confidence as you placed in him----"

"Is this observing my prohibition, Mr. Elmendorf?" said Jenny, stopping and facing him.

"Oh, well, possibly not."

"Then you will kindly say at once what your business is. I have told you I will not listen to anything you say about Mr. Forrest."

"I am detaining you here," he said, evasively. "Let us walk on."

"No, I will not walk on. Mr. Elmendorf, I have learned to look upon you as anything but a friend to me or mine, and I mean to be perfectly frank with you here and now. You have slandered my friend, you have tricked and misled my brother, you have deceived my mother, and I know well you have sought to injure me with my employer----"

"Oh, only so far as was justifiable in the protection of my own name. As your recommender and endorser for the position you hold, I had a right, when you showed yourself heedless of my counsel and defiant of my injunctions, to say to your immediate superior that he should be cautious about allowing your intimacy with Mr. Forrest to be prosecuted within the shelter of his sanctum and practically under his own nose. I----"

"That's quite enough, Mr. Elmendorf. You have added insult to injury. Once and for all, let there be an end of this. I decline any and all communication with you from this time on." And with cheeks that lacked no color now, and eyes all ablaze with wrath, Miss Wallen turned and left him. But Elmendorf pursued. He had one arrow left, and meant to send it home.

"At least I may accompany you to the corner, only twenty yards away, and there, as you suggest, our paths shall separate. You decline to believe my estimate of Mr. Forrest, and hold him up as something knightly and chivalric, forsooth. My deluded friend, all the time he was making you the object of those charming little attentions he was pressing his suit under my own eyes at home, and, in spite of all her father, her aunt, or her friends could do, I regret to say that Miss Florence Allison became so infatuated as to follow that young man to his exile, and should he ever return here it will doubtless be as her husband. Good-morning, Miss Wallen."

She had turned from him in renewed anger and disgust as they reached the corner, had hastened along with flaming eyes and cheeks and loudly throbbing heart. She was furious at him for daring to speak of such things, daring to couple Forrest's name with hers, with--anybody's. She was ready to cry out against the man for such malignity--mendacity; and then her cooler judgment and common sense began to reassert themselves. Why shouldn't it be true? Why shouldn't he seek the hand of one so--so lovely and wealthy as Miss Allison? What more natural than that Miss Allison should learn to love him? Why shouldn't she--she, Jenny Wallen--rejoice with her whole heart that her friend and protector could look forward to such happiness? He had never been anything but kind, thoughtful, courteous, to her. Other men had taken advantage of her defenceless post to accost her with low gallantries, with ***bourgeois*** flattery, with ridiculous attempts at flirtation or love-making, and she had laughed or stormed them off; but Forrest had shown her from the first the high-bred courtesy he would have accorded the proudest lady in the land, had never presumed upon a look, a word, a touch, that was not marked by respect and deference. He was a gentleman, she said; any girl might be proud of such a lover; and if it was true that he and Florence Allison were engaged, she would congratulate him and her with all her heart and rejoice with them and for them, and pray that their lives might be happy,--happy as her own was desolate,--and then the day became dark and dull and hopeless despite a brilliant sun, for just as the Lambert towers loomed in sight, the Allison carriage came spinning up the avenue, a radiant, happy, lovely face beaming upon her from the window, then turning to look up into the dark, soldierly features of the man at her side. Florence Allison was home, then, from her wanderings, bringing her beloved with her.

CHAPTER IX.

Elmendorf was an astonished man. He had confidently told Mrs. Lawrence that the objectionable lieutenant had been ordered off under a cloud of official censure and forbidden to return. He really believed it. It was one of his peculiarities that he invariably attached a sinister explanation to every action of his fellow men and women whose social station, at least, was superior to his own, when other explanation was withheld. He had sneeringly told Miss Wallen that unless the gentleman resigned from the army and returned to be the husband of Miss Allison, he would not return at all. He believed this too. He was so constituted mentally that he believed Forrest guilty of anything that could be alleged against him, believed that Miss Allison was interested in him to a certain extent, but would probably lose her interest when once the gallant himself was well out of the way, believed that he could even convince her, as he had convinced her aunt, that Forrest was totally unworthy her regard, provided Forrest himself did not return; and, lo and behold! Forrest had returned, and returned with Miss Allison herself, brought back on their train,--in their carriage, as he learned from Aunt Lawrence,--and apparently more influential with the father and daughter than ever before. Not until luncheon-time that day did he know of this, and the news came like a dash of ice-water on shivering skin. It was plain that Mrs. Lawrence looked to him to defend his statement and name his authorities then and there; for Miss Allison did not come down to luncheon, Cary was speedily excused and permitted to go about his own affairs, and then Mrs. Lawrence whirled upon the tutor with the tidings that not only was Mr. Forrest back, but that Florence had brought him back; that Mr. Allison, so far from objecting, had approved--had invited him to lunch with his fellow-magnates at the club and to dine *en famille* in the evening. As for Mr. Forrest being under the ban of official censure, Mrs. Lawrence declared she couldn't understand it, in view of the fact that he was with the general and his staff when the party encountered them at Wichita, and that the general himself had authorized his return to Chicago. "Authorized!" said Elmendorf, with his ready sneer; "*ordered*, very probably, with the view of having him tried by court-martial here where the witnesses are ready; and Mr. Forrest has had the effrontery to saddle himself on respectable company by way of establishing high connection to start with. I have heard of just such expedients before. My informants are men who thoroughly know the ins and outs of military affairs in the department, and they are not likely to be mistaken." All the same the tutor was glad to get away and to go post-haste to the Pullman building, hoping to catch his one intimate in the clerical force and to dodge the officials with whom he stood in evil odor. Luck often follows audacity. In the elevator he met two officers to whom he had been presented during the earlier days of his tutorship, when he was still cordially received. These gentlemen had been away on duty in the interim, and, knowing nothing of his lapse from grace, greeted him as pleasantly as ever, invited him into the aide-de-camps' offices, and there made him at home in the absence of the usual occupants. They knew nothing of Forrest's movements beyond the fact that he had not been with his regiment at all. One of the two was Major Cranston; the other was Lieutenant-Colonel Kenyon, of Forrest's own regiment. "I suppose you know he--left here under very sudden--rather summary, orders some two months ago," suggested Elmendorf; "and it created, as you can readily imagine, some little comment in society." No, Kenyon hadn't heard, and he eyed the speaker sharply from under his bushy, overhanging brows. Cranston, however, promptly replied that there was nothing in the least remarkable in it. Officers were frequently hurried off on sudden orders, and there was no reason why society should be exercised over it. Elmendorf promptly disavowed any intention of casting the faintest aspersion on Mr. Forrest, whom he at least had found to be certainly quite the equal of his comrades in most things pertaining to the officer and gentleman, although there were some things, perhaps, which to a humble civilian like himself might call for explanation. He was merely stating a fact, one which he regretted, of course, as he did all the idle talk that circulated in superficial circles of society. He was glad to find officers of such prominence as Kenyon and Cranston so ready to stand up for Forrest, as some men--he preferred not to mention names--had been less outspoken, at least, in his behalf. And then Kenyon impatiently arose and went out, Cranston met a brace of cavalrymen going back to their regiment after a leave, and Elmendorf drifted away in search of his clerk and found him.

A glance at the register showed that Forrest had already been in to report his arrival, had given his old rooms as his present address, and "verbal instructions of Dept. Comdr." as the explanation of his return. The adjutant-general, seated in his own office, had seen Forrest, and had further instructions to communicate, evidently, for they had been closeted together nearly half an hour, but what passed between them the clerk could not say, and Elmendorf was left to his own vivid imagination. Forrest certainly had not rejoined his regiment, and Elmendorf had chosen to think that that was what he was ordered to do when leaving Chicago. Thinking of it so much, he had come to believe it a fact; but Forrest was now back here in Chicago, as suddenly and mysteriously as he went. He was not, however, back in his old office, was not then restored to his functions at head-quarters. What more was needed, therefore, to warrant the belief that he was picked up by the general in his wanderings in the Indian Territory and sent in for trial on charges of disobedience of orders and absence without leave? At all events, it was a working theory in the absence of any other. Elmendorf strolled away discontentedly, and was presently overhauling books on Brentano's counters, and there Cranston found him, and, when books were the theme, found him more to his liking. They walked up to Cranston's old home that afternoon together, and Elmendorf, as previously detailed, made his first appearance before Mrs. Sergeant McGrath.

Later he strolled up to the Lambert Memorial, revolving many things in his mind. With all the discomfort and uneasiness and foreboding Forrest's sudden reappearance cost him, with all the embarrassment likely to follow, one reflection had given him joy. There at least within those walls was a proud and wilful girl whose spirit he had longed to tame, whose distrust and defiance he had smarted under, but who now would have to admit the truth of some of the most salient of his accusations and prophecies with regard to Forrest. There was still abundant opportunity for him to rejoice in that triumph. Wells did not like him, but what of that? Wells was probably gone by this time, and she would be there all alone, bending as usual over her typewriter. She couldn't order him out or refuse him admittance, since Wells had never yet done so. She would have to listen, and he would go and break to her the news of Forrest's return,--of Forrest's return with Florence Allison, of his luncheon with the magnates at the club to-day, of his coming to dinner informally, like one of the family, at the Allisons' to-night. It would be comfort to watch her sensitive face, thought Elmendorf, and he meant to make the successive announcements as humorous and lingering as his command of rhetoric would permit. His step was light, his smile significant, his bearing quite debonair, as he turned into the private hall-way and encountered the janitor at the first turn. The janitor was Irish. "Misther Wells is gone--if it's him ye want, sorr," said he, with scant civility, for the Celt had become imbued with distaste for the Teuton.

"Then I'll see his secretary," answered Elmendorf, with his usual shrug, and without a stop.

"Ye wouldn't, bedad, if I saw her first," said honest Maloney, as he looked after the agitator. "Maneness goes wid the loikes of him, and mischief and trouble wherever he sets his fut."

Springily did Elmendorf go up the echoing stairway, and then, reaching the second floor, he saw fit to saunter, and that, too, with noiseless footfall. He approached the familiar door-way, and the anteroom--the scene of his discomfiture when Donnelly presented Mart's liquor-bill--stood invitingly open. But the door to the private office beyond was closed, and it was barely five o'clock. She was there; he felt assured of that. He could hear the busy clicking of the typewriter. She was probably alone, too. Hitherto he had entered unannounced, but then the door stood open. Why should he knock now? He would not. He decided to enter as hitherto, and so, quietly, turned the knob and pushed.

But the door resisted. Evidently it was latched from within. Twice he made the trial, noiselessly as possible, and then paused to consider. This was something new. Miss Wallen had locked herself in, or possibly had locked him out. If not at her desk, she might easily have seen him sauntering leisurely up the street, might have seen him cross, and, divining that his object was to see her and perhaps renew his offensive talk, have taken prompt measures to resist. Well, even if lettered "Private Office" on the door, it was a public office in point of fact; and that public office was not for personal use or benefit he had the authority, in one sententious form or other, of many an Executive, from Jefferson down. So Elmendorf rapped, and rapped loudly. The clicking presently ceased, a light footstep was heard, then the voice of the official stenographer:

"What is wanted?"

"Open the door, please."

"Whom do you wish to see."

"I desire to speak with Miss Wallen."

"Miss Wallen declines."

"I have business to transact."

"Mr. Wells is not here, and Miss Wallen is not empowered to act for him. You will have to wait and see him to-morrow."

"Miss Wallen, you are barring me out of an office I have a perfect right to enter, and that I mean to enter here and now, or make formal complaint to the trustees. If this door is not opened in twenty seconds I warn you there will be trouble."

To this remark no answer whatever was vouchsafed. Miss Wallen quietly returned to her typewriter, and the only sound from within was the clicking of that ingenious machine. Elmendorf had sense enough not to shout his news, but he had not sense enough to abandon the attempt to tell her. There was another way of reaching the sanctum, provided he moved with promptness and decision. It was through the library itself. Turning away, muttering angrily, he returned through the darkening corridor, down the stairs, and around to the main entrance. Another moment, and he was at the lattice that separated the reading-room from the library proper. There, beyond, were the long aisles and rows of crowded shelves. Here was the customary throng of patrons, returning or taking out books. There were the busy attendants bustling to and fro, and beyond them and beyond those vaults and dim recesses was the passage leading to the sanctum of the head librarian. A young girl, standing within the lattice, was noting the numbers of some books upon a slip of card-board, and, with quick decision, Elmendorf addressed her. "Pardon me," said he, "I have to go into Mr. Wells's office at once. Miss Wallen has accidentally locked the door, and can't open it. Will you kindly let me through this way?"

The girl hesitated an instant. It was against orders, but she had often seen the gentleman in the library and in the sanctum itself with the librarian. "I suppose it will be all right," said she, doubtfully.

"Oh, certainly," said Elmendorf. "Pardon my haste; I have left some papers there that I need at once. Ah, thank you." And slipping through the wicket, he hastened on his way before any one else could interpose, and in another moment stood within the sanctum and closed the door behind him.

Nor was he much surprised to find Miss Wallen no longer at her instrument, but leaning wearily against the casement, apparently gazing out into the street. "You see," he began, with cold, sarcastic emphasis, "the power to lock one door does not make a woman the mistress of an entire situation. It would have been better had you accepted what was meant for your good and spared me the necessity of forcing it upon you, as it were; but I have had my own sisters to protect in the past, and knew what was best for you. Nor am I to be balked in what I consider my duty by the obstinacy of a moonstruck, passion-blinded girl."

She had turned her back upon him as he began to speak. Now she turned and faced him. He half expected fierce denunciation, but, to his surprise, her manner was as contemptuously cool as his was sardonically cold.

"You have succeeded in getting in here on the plea of business, Mr. Elmendorf; but this is insolence."

"It is my business, and has ever been and shall ever be, to stand between the helplessness of the poor and the oppression of the rich. My business is to see that you and yours suffer no wrong at the hands of those who consider such as you their natural prey. I see the ghost of a smile flickering about your lips, Miss Wallen, and am aware you regard my mission with disfavor, but you cannot and shall not treat it with contempt."

She was smiling, poor girl, and it was but the ghost of a wintry smile, too, for, even in her exasperation and distress, the whimsical, humorous side of her nature--its helpful, sunny side--was asserting itself at the moment. For the life of her she could not feel the indignation he deserved just then, for the contrast between the grandiloquence of his sentiments and the pettiness of that unpaid lodging-bill almost forced her to laugh outright.

"I am here," he went on, "because you would not believe my statements regarding Mr. Forrest, because I feel it my duty to open your eyes as to his character and intentions. You refused to believe what I said concerning him and you, and that only confirms my fears. I am powerless to contend against the logic of a woman's love, but when I spoke of him and her whom I may be pardoned for referring to as your rival, I spoke the truth."

Now she was smiling in contemptuous amusement again, as though she actually considered it beneath her to answer. How amazed would Miss Allison be at the idea of her being placed on the same plane with a working-girl!

Her silence and self-control maddened Elmendorf. "Have you no reason, no sense?" he demanded. "I told you this very day that she had gone to follow and bring him back, did I not?"

A cool nod of assent.

"I told you he would reappear here, if at all, only as her husband, or possibly her affianced, did I not?"

Another nod as cool as the first.

"And you turned away in contemptuous unbelief, did you not?"

"Contempt certainly, but unbelief--not entirely."

Elmendorf was fairly trembling with wrath by this time. The idea that this simple, unlettered, friendless "girl of the people" should so coolly brave him--him on whose words enraptured ears were wont to hang, at whose eloquence enthusiastic hundreds burst into applause! It stung him to the very marrow of his conceit. Something must be said or done to bring her to her knees, and, believing that she loved and dearly loved the man in question, he prepared his final *coup*.

"Well, it may modify your contempt to know that my words have come true."

"That Mr. Forrest was ordered away in disgrace?" she calmly asked.

"Not so much that, as that he has returned, brought back, as I said, by Miss Allison."

"Why, but that is no news at all. I knew he was coming, and I saw them together this morning."

"You--saw them--and you knew he was coming?" faltered the tutor. "You mean to--you mean he writes to you,--that you correspond with him?"

"I mean nothing whatsoever beyond what I said, Mr. Elmendorf,--that I knew Mr. Forrest would be here this week, that I saw them this morning; and, as it is his work that lies here unfinished, interrupted by this visitation, I may now, I presume, return to my business--and you to yours."

"Then he has been here, too?"

"Yes, and will be again,--another reason, perhaps, why you would better not linger. I will open the door now,--since it is to let you out."

"Yes, and to let him in, I suppose, and see him behind locked doors, as you doubtless have before, Miss Wallen----"

"The door is both unlocked and open, Mr. Elmendorf," said she, throwing it wide, but now in her turn the girl was quivering with indignation. "Furthermore, one touch on this button brings our janitor here--Mr. Wells speaks of him as 'our bouncer.'" And her white hand poised not six inches from the button.

Elmendorf took a long breath. "You may consider this a moral victory, Miss Wallen," said he, backing to the portal, "but you will do well to remember this. As I have said before, I have a duty to perform that I owe to society,--to my employers on the one hand, to the people on the other. Rest you well assured that whatever may have been his successes, so called, in the past, there are two schemes of your paragon, Mr. Forrest, that shall fail, even if I have to fight him through the public press. In one or other, separately, he may be too much for my efforts, but at one and the same time that accomplished *roue* shall never win a wife in that household and a mistress here."

And immediately thereafter a gentleman coming up the dim corridor without heard a sound that resembled the loud crack of a toy torpedo, followed by the reverberant bang of a door, and, a moment later, encountered an oddly familiar figure hurrying out and hanging on to its left jowl as though afflicted with a violent attack of *tic douloureux*.

"Why, I believe that's Mr. Elmendorf!" remarked the new-comer, and then was surprised to find the inner door locked,--to find that he had to knock thrice before it was opened, and by that time it seemed quite dark.

CHAPTER X.

The dinner at Allison's the night of his return from the long journey was not a success. It was to be an entirely informal affair,--no guests present but a high official of the road in which the host was so heavily interested, and Mr. Forrest, whom Miss Allison had invited on her own account. The brother magnate came, and Mr. Forrest did not. True, his acceptance had been conditioned on his being able to finish certain papers, which, so he told both Florence and her father, would be required at the office early the next day. Mr. Elmendorf came hurrying in and went up to his room about half-past six, and fifteen minutes later came a messenger with a note which was taken at once to Miss Allison's room. She was dressed for dinner and ready to come down, but she took it and read it hurriedly, uttered an exclamation of disappointment, and sharply closed her door. Not until Mr. Allison sent for her with the information that dinner was on the table did she appear. Elmendorf eyed her covertly, and Aunt Lawrence sharply. There were unmistakable traces of tears. "Did he say why he couldn't come?" asked Mrs. Lawrence, presently.

"Yes--no--at least--he had told me before that he thought it might be impossible," answered Florence, in embarrassment and annoyance. Her father was laying down the law on Interstate Commerce to his guest at the moment, and it was a subject on which he never tired. Even while listening intently, watching for his chance to "chip in," as Cary said, Elmendorf caught Miss Allison's every word. What he had not yet been enlightened upon was the explanation of Forrest's return with the party. All he knew was that early on the previous day the general, with two of his aides and Mr. Forrest, boarded the train in Southern Kansas. Allison invited them all into the private car and proposed making them his guests on the homeward run. The chief declined for himself and staff, saying that they had other matters to detain them, but it transpired that Mr. Forrest was to go right on. He had his berth engaged in an adjoining sleeper, but spent several hours with the railway party, and on their arrival in Chicago the Allisons had insisted on his taking a seat in their carriage. Allison himself was dropped at his club, Florence in turn left Mr. Forrest at his lodgings, and then was driven home. This was actually all Elmendorf had been able to learn.

But here was basis enough for all manner of theory and conjecture, none of them to Forrest's advantage, and Elmendorf felt that the more he could make of them the better for his own cause and the worse for Forrest. There had been an intangible something in Allison's manner to warn the tutor that just so soon as the guests were out of the way he might look out for squalls. Allison had greeted him with utter absence of cordiality, and Elmendorf felt that his employer was even more displeased with him than when he went away. Under such circumstances a wise man would have avoided saying or doing anything to augment the feeling against him, but Elmendorf, except in his own conceit, was far from wise, and his propensity for putting his foot in it was phenomenal. Allison loved his post-prandial cigar,--it agreed with him,--and so did his guest. The ladies withdrew quite early, Cary slipped away, and Elmendorf should have slipped after him, but here were two great men of the railway world, the natural oppressors of the masses, the very type of the creatures he delighted in describing upon the platform as "bloated bond-holders;" their conversation could hardly fail to be of interest to him, and he remained. Warming up to their work, they were discussing the situation at Pullman and its probable effect upon the employees of the roads centring in Chicago. That their views should be radically opposed to those of their absorbed listener was of course to be expected, and Elmendorf was fidgeting furiously upon his chair, every now and then striving to interject a sentence and claim the floor, but Allison knew his man, and knew that once started, Elmendorf could not well be suppressed. Every attempt on the part of the tutor to interpose, therefore, was met by uplifted and warning hand and prompt "Permit me" or "Permit Mr. Sloan to finish, if you please," which was galling in the last degree. Elmendorf had planned to have a conciliatory word or two with Miss Allison, with whom he knew himself to have been in grave disfavor ever since the occasion of his presuming to tender advice and remonstrance on the score of Mr. Forrest, but she had escaped to her own room again immediately after quitting the table. Her manner towards him showed that she had neither forgiven nor forgotten the impertinence, and that was additional reason why he should have done nothing more, in that household at least, to add to the array of his offences. But presently the opportunity came, and he could not resist. The Interstate Commerce Law was again under discussion. Allison had always fiercely opposed it, declaring it to be an utterly unconstitutional and unwarrantable interference with the rights of corporations and individuals. Mr. Sloan was rather more conservative. He was contending that, despite its restrictions upon certain railway companies, the appointment of the Commission had resulted in much that was beneficial to most parties concerned.

Allison burst forth impetuously: "Why, Sloan, look at the thing! It is direct and absolute usurpation on the part of the general government of the functions of the State. Here's a road running from Chicago to Cairo, for instance. Its traffic is entirely within the State; its offices, road-bed, and rolling-stock--everything concerning it, in fact--within the limits of the State; and yet, just because it delivers freight and passengers over on the Kentucky shore, here comes the general government formulating laws for its control, which should be the province of the State and of the State only. If we've got to be trammelled by legislation, let it be at the hands of our own legislators---- Eh, what?" he asked, breaking suddenly off to acknowledge the presence of the butler standing solemnly beside him with a card on the salver. Allison took the card mechanically, glanced at the name, and, even as he was saying, "Oh, show him in here. Send this up to Miss Florence," Elmendorf had seized his opportunity and "chipped in."

"Yes, but, my dear sir," he began, in his eager, nerve-racking, whining tone, "is there not inconsistency here? Can you deny that when the legislature, not only of this, but of neighboring States, essayed to enact laws on these very subjects, your attorneys were promptly on the ground to argue against it and to declare that only Congress had the power under the Constitution to regulate commerce between the States? Can you deny that at the meeting of managers and business-men here one of the most prominent of your number declared that you objected to any and all legislation? Can you deny that when Congress did take the matter up your attorneys were just as promptly in Washington, proclaiming that any attempt to legislate in your affairs was a violation of the rights of the sovereign States? Can you deny, in fine, that when the whole subject was under discussion here a second time, one of your most eminent **confreres** put himself on record as saying that, while he was opposed to any legislation, of two evils he preferred to choose the less, and if any legislators were to meddle with the affairs of the roads, better let it be the State Solons, who were far more--well--approachable and ready to listen to--let us say-- reason? Can you deny that----" But here Elmendorf found himself without listeners. The odd point in it all was that very much that he said was true; and Allison was reddening with wrath, and Sloan chuckling with suppressed merriment, when the entrance of a tall, brown-eyed, brown-moustached man in evening dress gave both opportunity to escape the deluge.

"Forrest at last!" exclaimed the host, turning and seizing his hand. "So sorry you were detained, lad; but sit you down, sit you down, and let me ring for some dinner for you. No? Had a bite? All right. Take a chair and some wine. Sloan and I were whacking away at the old bone."

"Yes, Allison, and here's a Federal officer who won't agree with you for a moment."

With a dissatisfied shake of his head, Elmendorf had arisen as though to pull his chair nearer the end of the table and resume his attack, but Allison had purposely turned his back squarely upon him and was drawing Forrest to the very place the tutor had hoped to occupy. Sloan arose and cordially shook hands with the newcomer, who then for the first time, apparently, caught sight of Elmendorf. The latter had started as though to come forward, but something in Forrest's eyes restrained him. The lieutenant simply bowed, and said, very coldly, "Good-evening," but did not even mention the tutor by name.

"Now, Mr. Forrest," began Mr. Sloan, with much heartiness of manner, "I want you to say to Allison here just what you said to me. He's a trifle hot-headed to-night. He thinks the government has been paternalizing at our expense, and that only harm will come from it."

Forrest looked from one to the other a moment, a quiet smile upon his lips. All the previous afternoon as they trundled along in the cosy private car had these gentlemen been disputing over the same thing, and late in the evening, as Mr. Sloan and Forrest were enjoying a cigar together, they, too, had had a chat upon the subject, and Sloan had turned and looked upon the officer in some surprise. In common with most of his class, the man of wealth and worldly wisdom had regarded the *genus* regular officer as a something impressive, possibly, on parade, useful probably on the frontier, but out of place anywhere else. That he should have read or studied anything beyond drill and dime novels was not to be expected. The magnates had even had their modest game of draw poker at a late hour and laughingly referred some mooted question to Forrest as a probable expert, and were astonished to hear that he had never played, not so much because he disapproved of it as because he had never had time. Allison had already found out that Forrest was a student and a thinker, but up to that evening he was the only man of the party who believed that the average officer had any other use for time than to kill it. Whatever it was that

Mr. Forrest might have said to Mr. Sloan, it was evident he did not care to repeat it now.

"I would rather not reopen the matter," said he. "Possibly I had no right to forecast the action of the government, even speculatively, in a contingency that may not arise."

Elmendorf planted his chair and lighted a cigarette, throwing himself down with an air as much as to say, "Well, I've got to be bored and must be resigned to it, since they won't listen to a man of intelligence;" and Allison, with blacker gloom in his eyes, looked squarely at him as he began to speak:

"Sloan, you're not even sipping your wine; Forrest, you never seem to indulge. Suppose we three adjourn to my den, where the books are right at hand. Mr. Elmendorf has his duties and will excuse us."

If he had struck him, the master of the house could not more have stung his employee. Even Forrest, who by this time had many reasons of his own for bringing Elmendorf to book, tingled with something like sympathy at a slight so marked. There were so many other and better ways of letting Elmendorf know that in the coming conference his presence could be dispensed with, that Sloan spoke of it the moment they reached the library; but Allison was imperious and positive. "You don't begin to know the man," said he. "Anything less than unmistakable prohibition he would consider as invitation, and he'd turn our talk into a lecture on the relations of capital to labor. You saw how he got in the instant I stopped a moment, Sloan."

"Faith and I did," said Sloan, laughing, "and he hit you fellows in the ribs. Why, where'd he find it all out?"

"I'm blessed if I know, unless it was from the newspaper men. They get hold of almost everything,--wrong side foremost, as a rule, but they get it. Now I heard something of your talk last night. Brooks was speaking of it. He looks upon the Interstate Bill just as I do. What do you mean by saying it might prove our salvation?" he asked, abruptly, turning to Forrest.

"I was simply supposing a case," said Forrest, calmly. "Say that the Granger element in one State, the Populists in another, the Socialists in a third, were to obtain control of the legislature and elect their own governor. You say they are utterly antagonistic to the railways; that in the event of a general strike, mob violence, etc., they would refuse you help or protection; that as common carriers you would be powerless to carry out your contracts, and that not only passenger and freight traffic would be blocked, but the government mails. Now, prior to February, '87, the general government, as I understand it, had left the management of the railways to the States. It had neither formulated laws for their control nor adopted measures for their protection. In the great railway riots of '77, when the police and militia were whipped and cowed by the mobs, such States as Pennsylvania and Illinois begged for government aid and got it. Our troops were called in from the Rocky Mountains to Chicago, and from Louisiana to Pittsburg. In the riots at Buffalo, three years ago, New York's fine National Guard, and in those at Homestead the Pennsylvania division, were sufficient to put an end to the mischief, and neither State had to ask for help; but here lies within your limits far greater possibility for riot and bloodshed than can be found elsewhere in the Union, and suppose that to pander to the masses here, as he has done in pardoning the Anarchists, your governor should deny you protection and permit assault, riot, and violence whenever you attempted to move engines or trains. It is my belief that you can now look where you could not before the passage of that Interstate Commerce Bill in '870 for the protection denied you at home. When the Congress of the United States enacted that 'every common carrier should, according to their respective powers, afford all reasonable, proper, and equal facilities for the interchange of traffic between their respective lines,'--I am quoting now,--'and for receiving, forwarding, and delivery of passengers and property to and from their several lines,' the supreme power of the land asserted its right to assume control over all roads except those doing business exclusively within the limits of some one State; and when the general government says to a common carrier that it must do this or must not do that, it means that the general government will back it in carrying out its orders; and whether it be mails, passengers, live stock, perishable goods, time freight or construction trains, the railway companies can now look to the United States for protection, whether any individual State likes it or not. You have abused that law as a menace to your rights as a business-man, Mr. Allison. You may live to bless it as all that stood between you and anarchy."

Forrest had spoken in a quiet, conversational tone, noting that Allison had closely eyed the heavy folds of the portiere, and once, stepping quickly thither, had drawn it aside and glanced about him; but the tutor had vanished, if that was what he was looking for. When Forrest stopped, Sloan turned to his friend with a merry twinkle in his eyes. "How's that for Federalist doctrine as opposed to States' rights, Allison? I expect to hear you saying, 'Almost thou persuadest me to be a Federalist,' before Forrest is done with you."

"Well, I certainly never looked for such an interpretation of the law. It has only been a bother, a nuisance, a senseless trammel upon us thus far, interfering with all our business, breaking up our long-haul and short-haul tariffs, requiring us to account practically to the government for every penny we charge and almost every one we expend. Do you mean this is the way the law is looked upon at head-quarters?" he asked, glancing keenly at the soldier.

"I have no means of knowing how the general understands it," said Mr. Forrest, simply. "The matter may be tested before we think possible. I understand that the condition of these poor people at Pullman is getting worse every day, and that there is wide-spread sympathy for them among the wage-workers everywhere; and I don't wonder at it."

"Why, they've only themselves to blame, Forrest. They seem to have done no laying up for a rainy day. They had good homes and good wages so long as business boomed, and they have spent just as freely as they got the money. Now there's no business for the company, no orders for cars, not enough to keep them going. No man can expect a company to run its business at a loss; and yet these people kick because they can't have the same wages they were getting when work was brisk."

"Well, now, is that strictly so, Mr. Allison? I have talked with these people. I have been told by them, quiet, conservative, well-informed Pullman men, that they concede that the wages must come down, and that all hands will have to retrench awhile until better times. They are willing to do that and stand by their company. But, on the other hand, they think, and I think, the company owes something to them. Here are honest, capable, intelligent fellows who have served the company fifteen and twenty years, have reared families within its walls, occupied its houses, and paid its rents. They may not have saved, I admit, but they have *served* faith-fully and long and well. They have never failed in their obligation to the company, and prompt payment of wages is not the only duty of a corporation to its people. The company is wealthy. It is even declaring a dividend. None of its salaries have been cut down as a consequence of the business depression. It has simply said to its wage-workers, 'You alone are the ones to suffer. You and your families and your cares and troubles are nothing to us. Here's the difference between your last month's wages and your last month's rent. Next month there'll be no wages to speak of, but we'll expect the rent all the same.' In my opinion, that company is losing the chance of winning the love and gratitude of thousands of men and women whose affection is worth a good deal more than all the money they'll ever save this way. It would have been an easy thing to say, 'We'll bear our share of the burden. These are hard times, and we've had to cut down your wages until the dawning of a better day; we'll cut the rents down, too.'"

"Forrest, that's Utopia," said Mr. Allison.

"I admit it, but I know something of these people, Mr. Allison. The past year perhaps has done more to open my eyes than all those which have preceded. I have seen something of the struggles, the self-denial, the charity, the patience, the help-fulness, of the working classes. I have learned a feeling of respect and sympathy for those who are the workers that is exceeded only by the contempt I feel for the drones and for those whom they hail as their advisers."

"Like our----, for instance," said Allison, uplifting his eyes as though to include the study aloft.

"Well, I know less of him or his speeches, perhaps, except by vague report, than of others who are prominent. They are preaching a doctrine that can only make matters worse for the laborer. They counsel strike, and forcible, riotous resis-tance to the employment of others. It can lead only to tumult, to rioting that brings out the criminal and the desperate classes; outrage results, and the sympathy they might have received goes against them. Their very worst enemies are these men who are posing as strike-leaders."

"Well, what do you think of the prospect? Does it look like an outbreak?" asked Mr. Sloan.

"To me, yes, for every day makes the suffering worse at Pullman, and the com-pany refuses to hear of arbitration. From a purely business point of view I cannot deny their right to do so, but the very attitude assumed by the corporation makes many of the labor-leaders' accusations true. The company has not contracts enough for new cars to keep all hands employed on full time and full wages, perhaps. Many of its employees are single men, comparatively new at the business; they can afford to be frankly told to go elsewhere in search of work; but to hold everybody while scaling the wages of all hands, month after month, down, down until a family man cannot pay his rent and feed his children, then the cord breaks. Just or unjust, the impression prevails among the railway men everywhere I have been that the Pullman Company has made vast sums, that it is about the only company not actually losing money now, and that it is protecting itself through a bad year by heavily taxing its people. There have been sympathetic strikes before; what if one should be ordered now?"

"That's the enormity of the whole business," broke in Mr. Allison. "What I wish could be done with our hands would be to have them regularly enlisted for the work,--so many years unless sooner discharged,--just like the soldiers, by Jove! Then when a man quit work it would be desertion, and when he combined with others to strike it would be mutiny. Ah, we'd have a railway service in this country then that would beat the world."

Forrest smiled. "Rather too much like a standing army controlled by corporation that would be; and a standing army is a luxury the Constitution forbids even to sovereign States. Besides, would men enlist in such a service?"

"Well, how do *you* get them, then? The Lord knows you treat them worse than we do."

"The Lord might believe that if he knew nothing but what the papers say," answered Forrest, half laughing. "But in point of fact we don't begin to work our men as you do, and we give them far more for their work. Another thing: our workman knows just what he is going to get from month to month, and he signs his contract to accept such bounty, pay, rations, etc., as may be provided by law. No corporation can scale him down ten, twenty, thirty, or fifty per cent. when times are hard; it takes the Congress of his country to do that; and when, as once happened, Congress did adjourn without appropriating a cent for our pay, the whole army stood by its obligation, because it knew the people would stand by it next term. That, by the way, was the year you railway men had most urgent need of its aid,--'77. But," said Forrest, suddenly starting to his feet, "here I have been inflicting a half-hour's monologue, and--I had hoped to see Miss Allison."

"You have fed Allison some truths that will do him good, if he can only digest them," said Mr. Sloan, whimsically, "and put me up to some things I'm glad to hear.

Was that what took you off so hurriedly and kept you away so long,--investigating the feeling of the railway hands all over the West?"

"No, indeed," said Forrest, promptly. "It was a very different thing."

"By the way, Forrest, that reminds me," said Allison, with a grin on his face, as he touched his bell to summon the butler, "you've never told us what did take you off, and my sister has been consumed with scandal or something about it. She began at me this afternoon. I told her to apply to you for particulars." **Bang** again on the bell, also "Damn that butler! He's never around after nine o'clock. I believe he goes to sleep."

A quick step through the drawing-room and parlor. The folds of the portiere were drawn aside, and Elmendorf stood revealed. "The butler stepped out a moment ago, sir. I met him at the front. Can I summon any one else for you?"

Allison's face showed added annoyance. "No. Unless--at least---- Is Miss Florence in the parlor?"

"Miss Allison some time since, sir, begged to be excused."

"Isn't she well?" asked Allison, looking at the tutor in some amaze.

"I cannot say as to that, sir. Miss Allison was in conversation with her aunt awhile."

"Odd," said Allison, irritably. "These women are queer. Excuse me a moment, will you?" And, rising, he left the room.

They felt, rather than heard, that he had gone up to make his own inquiries. His voice presently was audible, growling in his sister's boudoir. Elmendorf had disappeared and gone they knew not whither.

"Well, it's time for me to be off," said Sloan, consulting his watch, "yet I don't want to leave without saying good-night."

"As for me, I have to go," said Forrest, "because of an engagement."

"Oh, you can go any time, as you merely dropped in to call on the ladies; but I dined here. Now---- Excuse me, Mr. Forrest, I've only known you a day or two, but you've interested me, so to speak. You stick to Allison, and you'll be of infinite use to him in case of trouble here. He gets off his base sometimes. Stick to him, my lad, and your fortune's made."

Ten minutes later, when John Allison, with vexation and trouble on his brow, came down to the library, his guests were gone. A few lines on a card explained.

Each had engagements. "No wonder," said Mrs. Lawrence, joining him presently. "I know what his engagement is, and Mr. Forrest seemed to know what was coming."

Impatiently, irritably, the master of the house turned away. "I want to hear no more of this. Of course, if it's true, I shall know how to act. I'll--I'll go to the library in the morning, early."

This he did, and apparently to some purpose, for when he saw Mr. Forrest at the club at noon he turned his back upon him and moved quickly away.

CHAPTER XI.

During the week that followed, Mr. Elmendorf seemed to tread on air and bask in sunshine and favoring breeze. When returning from the trip, Allison had almost made up his mind to get rid of him. Now, while at the bottom of his heart he felt that he liked, and suspected that he trusted, him less than ever, Allison found himself powerless to carry out his intention. In the first place, Cary was certainly behaving better than he had behaved in long months before: Aunt Lawrence vouched for that. She deplored only the fact that he seemed unable now to fix his ambition on any other career than the army. Still, even doting and distracted parents have been known to cherish such an ambition long months at a time, and to stimulate it by promises of "working all possible wires" to secure the much-desired cadetship. Then if it couldn't be had they were just so much ahead: the boy had been weaned from evil habits and associations through his longing to enter the army. That he should have been disappointed at the last was through no fault of theirs, even though it gave them secret joy. They were doubly the gainers. Had the father stopped to think, he would perhaps have seen that Cary's steadiness and studious ways were all due to this new and consuming desire and to the advice of his friends at head-quarters; but Allison had many cares and worries now, and could only thank heaven, and perhaps, as Aunt Lawrence suggested, Elmendorf, that such reformation had been achieved in his boy.

But never until the evening of his return had he seriously faced the problem as to Forrest for a son-in-law. Only once or twice had he vaguely asked himself if there was danger of Flo's falling in love with him. With parental fondness he looked upon it as quite natural that Forrest should fall in love with her, and with worldly wisdom thought it more than probable that Forrest should desire to become possessed of so many charms and concomitant stocks and bonds. All that made no serious difference. Forrest might love and languish all he liked, if it was fun for Flo. It never occurred to him that her father's daughter could fall in love on her own account with a penniless lieutenant. But now he and Aunt Lawrence had had a sharp talk. Florence was not to go down, said she, and it was time her brother knew why. The child was infatuated with a man unworthy of her from almost every point of view, yet who, while paying her lover-like devotions, dared to slight her at times for a--creature with whom he was maintaining relations that needed to be promptly investigated and put an end to. He, that man Forrest, had dared to send a note to Florence Allison excusing himself from dinner on the plea of urgent work that had to be finished, and then was seen in a public place supping with the low-bred person herself. Yes, since Allison demanded to know, Mr. Elmendorf *was* her informant. But ask anybody at the Hotel Belmont, where the two brazenly appeared together at the very hour Forrest was due here. It wasn't a block from the library. Then ask the janitor of the Lambert who were there in the private office afterwards, and, though he is here now, see if from here Forrest does not go back to her, back to that same office where so often they have been closeted before this. Mrs. Lawrence had been compelled, she said, to open Florence's eyes as to this deceit and duplicity of her lover, and naturally she had declined to go downstairs and receive him. She did not say, however, that Florence had indignantly refused at first to believe that there was anything wrong, had worked herself up into a glorious passion of tears over the matter, and was looking like a fright in consequence when, full twenty minutes after its arrival, Mrs. Lawrence pushed Forrest's card under the locked door of her niece's room. Elmendorf had slipped out twice during the evening, was in and out like a flitting shadow, and on each return had brought Mrs. Lawrence new and more significant tidings. Florence had bathed her face and done all she could to make herself presentable, and was preparing to go down, when informed that Forrest was gone. And later that night Mrs. Lawrence deluged her, as she had her brother, with the details of Forrest's scandalous doings.

Wells was out when Allison visited the library the following morning, but the janitor was on hand to do reverence to the great director and trustee. "Who was in the private office last night, Maloney?" said he, sternly. And, distressed to think that anybody could suppose he'd allow any one there who had no business, Maloney promptly answered, "Sure nobody, sorr, barrin' Miss Wallen and Mr. Forrest. He come back twice and took her home. Misther Elmendorf was here, sorr----" But Allison did not wait to hear about him. Seated at her desk when he entered, Jenny promptly arose in respect to the distinguished arrival, but he merely growled an inquiry for Mr. Wells, looked her sharply over, and banged out again, leaving the poor girl with vague sense of new trouble to add to the weight of care she was already bearing. As he tramped away down town, Allison told himself he was not sorry that he had so crushing a piece of circumstantial evidence with which to demolish Forrest's aspirations, yet down in the depths of his heart he knew he was sorry, for he had grown to like him well. Just what course to pursue he had not determined. He would see Wells, see the Hotel Belmont people, see one or two parties referred to by Mr. Elmendorf as "highly respectable and responsible" who could tell him far more in the same strain, then see his brother trustees and dispose of Miss Wallen's case. Meantime, Florence was kindly, affectionately urged not to see Mr. Forrest in the event of his calling. And so Elmendorf's schemes were working grandly. He could well afford now to let them seethe and bubble. He could hold his peace and position at home, give renewed attention to those grander projects for the elevation of the down-trodden and the down-treading of the elevated, keep out of Forrest's way, and occupy himself in the cultivation of his new acquaintance Major Cranston, in the enjoyment of the privileges accorded him in Cranston's library, and in the incidental conversion to the true political faith of those dyed-in-the-wool devotees to Cranston's service,--iniquitous, feudalistic, slave-like service Elmendorf deemed it,--old Sergeant McGrath, his better half, and the nephew.

And while he was in the midst of this, came other helping hands. Florence Allison's social friends were prompt to hear of her return and of her bringing with her the objectionable aspirant, and were equally prompt to call in eager shoals. Somewhere the impression had got abroad that her army friend had been ordered off under a cloud, and, though no one at head-quarters could explain it, many society people could, and entirely to their own satisfaction. The men who knew Forrest liked him, but few women seemed to know him at all. After standing a social siege of some forty-eight hours, even Miss Allison's nerves gave way, and she had to deny herself to callers. In the midst of the speculation and sensation ensuing at the moment came the news that once more, suddenly and without the faintest explanation, Mr. Forrest had left Chicago. "I deeply regret your illness and that I was unable to see you to-day," he wrote from the club to Miss Allison, "but I am ordered away on duty that may cover several weeks, and have not a moment to spare. Tell Cary for me that I will leave with my landlady the books I promised him. I would urge his reading them carefully. With my regards to Mr. Allison and Mrs. Lawrence, believe me, Yours faithfully." And this was only four days after the luckless dinner. Florence ministered to the consuming curiosity of her aunt and showed her the letter, but the adjutant-general at head-quarters was less considerate; even society reporters could extract from him no hint as to why or where Lieutenant Forrest had gone. But that only served to stimulate conjecture and suggestion; and, to gossips born, a little stimulant goes, like the stories it sets afloat, long leagues beyond hope of recapture.

Then there were some lonely, anxious days for a pale-faced, slender, sad-eyed girl who seemed to get no benefit from the bracing breezes, and then, bursting suddenly from winter to summer, as is often the way with our ill-ordered, turbulent, defiant, and generally indescribable climate, came the first day of moisture-laden heat, depressing, debilitating,--a day when the tide of his affairs swept Elmendorf from his moorings at Cranston's and sent the freeholder thereof in search of a stenographer,--the day when poor Jenny begged to be excused from having even to write that detested name. And then speedily came the long-threatened outbreak, the demand of the American Railway Union that the public cease to patronize or the railway companies to run, no matter what their contracts, the cars of the Pullman Company. "We've got 'em by the throat at last," screamed Mart Wallen at Donnelly's Shades that night. "This means that the people, the people of the whole nation, have risen to down that damned old miser, and we'll make a clean sweep of other misers while we're about it."

"We've got 'em foul," echoed with drunken hiccoughs the graceless nephew Mrs. Mac and her sobered sergeant were dragging home between them, deaf to the eloquence of Elmendorf haranguing the crowd in the open square beyond. What was he saying?--"Stand firm, and the blood of the innocent victims of the glorious appeal of seven years ago, the martyred lives of the innocent men who died upon the scaffold, strangled in their effort to speak for you and your children, not only will not have been lost in vain, but soon shall be magnificently avenged. Oh, that it had been my lot to lead you here in '86! God be thanked, it is my lot to lead you now!"

"Oh, that ye had been here to lead in '86, ye howling lunatic," echoed Mrs. Mac, shaking her one unoccupied fist at the glorified but luckily distant face of the speaker; "yer only lot this night would have been in the graveyard, for ye never would have lived to lead anything, barrin' yer own funeral."

CHAPTER XII.

Then came a few days in which Elmendorf was in his glory. To be in a position where he could command attention, where he could practically compel people of all classes and conditions to be his listeners, to hang upon his words and regard him as clothed with power backed by authority, this was indeed joy and triumph new to him, though still far below the dreams he had dreamed. Though not even a member of the great railway union, not even possessing the confidence of its leaders, the fervor of his speeches had won him favor and admitted him to their councils. Not even tolerated for days at head-quarters, he suddenly reappeared there with all the assurance of the past, and during the first forty-eight hours of the memorable strike no one man in all Chicago seemed to carry on his shoulders the weight of information, authority, and influence of John Allison's whilom tutor, whose note of dismissal, unopened, awaited him at the deserted study. To the officials of the American Railway Union he represented himself as deep in the confidence of the officials at military head-quarters, personally intimate with most of the staff, and a man to whose warnings the general himself ever lent attentive ear. To the adjutant-general and others in authority, the chief being still away, he declared himself the envoy of the leaders of the strike, a man empowered to levy war or compass peace. In both assumptions he was impudent, yet not without support. What he craved was prominence, notoriety, the fame, if not the fact, of being an arbiter in the destinies of Chicago in this crisis of her history. From the Pullman to the Leland, from inner depot to outlying freight-yards, from meetings to municipal offices, he sped, never stopping for rest or refreshment. Irascible officers at Springfield, receiving despatches signed Elmendorf, put an H to his name and lopped it off at the neck. There were two precincts he left unpenetrated,--the head-quarters of the railway managers and those of the National Guard. Allison had made him known at the one, his public utterances and persistent sneers at "the militia boys," "our tin sol-dier boys," at the other. His appearance in the armory of any regiment in the city would have been the signal for a demonstration he had no desire to face. Through the newspaper offices, too, he flitted, shedding oracular statement and prophecy, claiming to speak "by the card" when he had news to tell, and preserving mysteri-ous, suggestive silence when questioned on matters whereof he knew nothing.

Two days had the strike been in force. Switchmen, yardmen, firemen, had quit their posts, and they or sympathizing gangs of toughs stoned and cursed the men who took their places. Yard-masters and master-mechanics leaped into the cabs and handled the levers of switch-engines; white-handed clerks and electricians swung lanterns and coupled cars; conductors turned switchmen, superintendents became conductors, and managers stepped down to yard-masters; and still the mob, gaining in numbers and wrath and villany with every hour, blackguarded the trainmen, blockaded the trains, and bombarded with sticks and stones and coupling-pins the few shrinking and terrified passengers. Trains reaching the city were towed in with every pane smashed and their inmates a mass of cuts and bruises. Trains due in the city and seized by the strikers were side-tracked at desolate prairie stations miles from food and water, and helpless, pleading women and children were penned up in them and left to hunger and thirst and tremble. In vain the railway officials pleaded with the city authorities for protection for passengers and trains. "We have been watching everywhere; we've seen no violence," was the answer. Policemen along the railway lines laughed and looked on while, almost within swing of their clubs, strikers were kicking a victim to death. In vain all appeals to the State. This was a popular movement,--a poor man's protest against the tyranny of a grasp-ing monopolist,--The People *vs.* Pullman. Let the railways join in and discard his cars, and all would be well. Contracts be damned! What cared they for the law of contract when on the eve of revolution--and election? Feigning to believe that the managers were merely pretending that their roads were blocked, openly asserting

that the managers could run their trains if they really wanted to, and slyly intimat-
ing that all the destruction thus far effected was at the hands of paid emissaries of
the managers themselves, officials of a great State and of a great city, sworn to preserve peace and good order and enforce the laws, dared to look idly on and trust the
masses, to whom they betrayed the honor of the commonwealth, for the vindication of a re-election. Within three days of the start, passenger traffic, except on the
two or three roads in the hands of the Federal courts, was practically ended, freight
traffic paralyzed, and the great stock-yards were in the hands of a mob of frantically
rejoicing men. "Not one wheel shall turn in any yard in all Chicago with the morrow's sun," said Elmendorf, slyly and jeeringly exultant in the presence and hearing
of officers and clerks at the Pullman building late that night. "The managers have
played their last card, made their last bluff. The State and the city virtually tell them
that it is their own fight, with their own men, men whom they have systematically
browbeaten, bullied, swindled, and starved until now the worm has turned. At last
you see the beginning of the end, the dawn of the glorious future, the rise of labor
against capital, and your friends the magnates have the option of ruin or surrender. I
tell you, gentlemen, three hundred thousand freemen will line those tracks at noon
to-morrow, and if their----" But the officers to whom he addressed himself turned
impatiently away. Clerks were passing to and fro along the hall between the office
of the adjutant-general and their desks. Some powerful but subdued excitement
pervaded the building. Watchers of the strikers had noted the increasing number of
officers in civilian dress long after the usual business hours, and Elmendorf, quick
to take the alarm, had hastened thither to ferret out the cause. Vain his effort to
communicate with his one victim. He was at his desk, and a vigilant ex-sergeant-
major of cavalry scowled at the would-be intruder and told him visitors could not
enter the clerks' rooms. Vain his effort to extract news along the corridors. No man
seemed to know why so many of them were there. Perplexed, he rushed back to
his associates, the strike-leaders. "Are you sure they're stanch at Springfield?" he
asked; "sure they haven't asked for aid from Washington?" The idea was laughed to
scorn.

"The governor is with us to the bitter end," was the loud boast of prominent
sympathizers, "and until he touches the button no power in or out of Illinois can
stand between us and victory. To-morrow we lock the lines from Pittsburg to the

Pacific."

Exultant, he sprang into a cab and drove to the north side. It was late at night, but he had his latch-key. A bath, a few hours' rest, a change of linen, and he would issue forth on the morrow refreshed, invigorated, ready to launch his shallop on this tide in his affairs which, taken at full flood, must lead to everlasting fame and fortune. Who would now dare crush him with curt refusal to listen? Who would pooh-pooh his prophecies, who deny his views, who withhold the homage due him now, as he strode, agitator, elevator, inspirer, ***Anax andron***,--King of men,--the divinely appointed, heaven-anointed leader of mankind in this sublime movement for liberty and the Lord only knew what else? It was late, and the great house was dark, but he let himself in, and, seeking first the butler's pantry, ransacked the larder for refreshment. He had eaten and drunk his fill, when the electric bell called his eye to the indicator. Some one at the street door. Humming softly his blithe tune, he shuffled over the tiled pavement and unbolted the inner door. A telegraph-boy handed him two messages, with a receipt-book and pencil. "John Allison," was all he said.

"I don't think he's home," said Elmendorf. "Did you try the club?"

For answer the boy sleepily pointed with grimy finger to the address on the envelope. Street and number were distinct.

"Well, just wait, youngster, and I'll see if he's in," said Elmendorf, and trotted swiftly, noiselessly up-stairs. Mr. Allison's room was open, the gas burning dimly at the toilet-table, but no one was there. Even as he hesitated what to do, a door at the east end of the wide corridor quietly opened, and a flood of light from Miss Allison's boudoir shot across the darkness. Elmendorf heard the soft rustle of silken folds, and hastened towards the light. Florence stood there at the door-way in some rich wrap of a pale, delicate shade of pink. Billows of creamy lace broke away from the shoulders and down along the entire front. The short elbow-sleeves seemed to burst into creamy foam, while a band of sable fur encircled and contrasted with the pure white throat, and was caught at the back by a knot of ribbon. It was one of her Parisian purchases, a modern conceit, something she never wore except in her own room or Aunt Lawrence's, but Elmendorf looked upon her with a glow of admiration in his keen, eager eyes that even in her hour of anxiety and fatigue she could not fail to notice and resent.

"If you have messages for my father, I will take charge of them," she simply said.

"Er--pardon me. I was about to offer my services, Miss Allison, as these may be immediate. If you will tell me where Mr. Allison is to be found----"

"I will not trouble you," she answered, coldly, and the plump white hand, extended for the messages, was the only thing about her that did not seem to turn from him in dislike.

Flushed with the triumph of the two days gone, intoxicated, possibly, by the dreams of his own dawning greatness, Elmendorf refused to accept rebuff. Who was she to treat with scorn the man whose merest word now could move a million stalwarts! "You must pardon me, Miss Allison," he answered, with emphasis. "I am not here in the capacity of a menial in the household. The events of the past few days have conspired to make me a factor in affairs, with power and influence far exceeding that wielded by my late employer. Furthermore, I should see him, or rather he should seek to see me, within the next few hours, unless he has resigned himself to the crash which must involve all he holds priceless in business and may even involve all he holds precious here."

"May I trouble you for those despatches, Mr. Elmendorf?" she asked, wearily, almost disgustedly.

Elmendorf flushed with wounded vanity. "The despatches are yours," he said, bowing with marked reverence. "But, as this may be my last opportunity of speaking to you in some days, I have that to say which I urge you for your own sake, your brother's sake, your father's sake, to hear and heed. On many occasions I have conscientiously striven to point out to your honored, if somewhat opinionated, sire the injustice, indeed I may say the brutality, of the views he so openly expresses towards the labor class. He has not received my advice in the kindly spirit in which it was offered, but, as possibly you know, matters have come to a climax, and such is the gravity of the situation that not only is his property in jeopardy, but his life. Nay, I know you have not forgiven me for words spoken only through motives of the most loyal and honorable devotion to your best interests. I see this bores you; but, Miss Allison, let me say to you in so many words that if the P.Q. & R. road persists in its refusal to restore those trainmen who were discharged yesterday for side-tracking a Pullman car at Grand Crossing, your father's life may be the forfeit."

"And yet the strike-leaders declare there is no violence, and that the strikers will commit none," she said, wearily.

"That was the spirit with which they entered upon this controversy; but when the managers persisted in hiring men to fill their places, and even dared to discharge employees for no worse crime than sympathy with their own brothers, even they who have listened to and obeyed me in the past murmur and threaten now. It will take my uttermost--as it shall be my sweetest--effort to stand between you and harm----"

But here the pink corded silk swished disdainfully about, its Watteau pleat flashed out of sight through the door-day, and that portal was slammed in the speaker's face. The mover of multitudes found himself alone in the darkened hall, snubbed and wrathful. Cary's room was just above, and the tutor smiled sardonically as, peering in there, he saw the boy lying half dressed upon his bed, covered by a Navajo blanket that Forrest had given him on his birthday, a revolver on the chair. A moment later, in his own room, he found pinned on his toilet-table a note addressed in Allison's well-known hand. It was a curt dismissal from his service, subject to the stipulated "one month's notice," and an intimation that in the interim his services and his presence could both be dispensed with. No reason was assigned, though the teeming columns of the press contained reason more than enough.

"Turned out like a dog," he snarled. "Let us see what they'll say in the morning."

And then he started and listened, for down on the floor below, light hurried foot-falls sped along the corridor. It was Florence hastening to her father's room. Stealthily Elmendorf sprang to the landing without, leaned over the balustrade, and bent his ear. He heard the unmistakable r-r-r-ing of the telephone bell,--Allison's own room, too. Then he had had to yield one pet prejudice at least as a result of the wide-spread influence of the strike. "He'll have to yield to more than that," said Elmendorf.

"Give me 332,--quick, please," he heard her call, her voice tremulous with excitement. That was not Allison's office; that was not the club nor the managers' association. Where then was he? What scheme was afoot? Hist! "Is that the superintendent's office P.Q. & R.?" she asked, "Is Mr. Allison there--Mr. John Allison? No? Where? Down at the depot? Please send for him at once to come to the 'phone.

Say his daughter has despatches for him of the utmost importance. Yes, I'll hold the line."

Silence for a long, long minute. Elmendorf could hear his heart thumping loud. What on earth could Allison be doing at the depot of the P.Q. & R. at one in the morning? The tracks of the road in a dozen places between the station and the suburbs were piled high with wrecked freight-cars at nine o'clock. The beautiful Silver Special, scheduled to leave each night at eleven-thirty, had been stalled there since the strike began, yet rumor had it that the management meant to launch it southwestward, mails, express, buffet, chair-car, and sleepers complete, if they had to cram its roofs and platforms with deputies armed with Winchesters. Could it be that already wrecking-trains were clearing a passage, and that this hated train, the reddest rag that could be flaunted in the face of the raging bull of the strike, was to burst the blockade and cover the strikers with derision? Perish all thought of sleep or change of linen! That station was a long three miles away, but he could get there, and to the haunts of the strikers farther beyond. But first he must hear the purport of those despatches. Now--her voice again!

"Yes. What is it? Oh, papa? Can you hear me?--distinctly? Then listen. Here are two despatches, the first from Washington--Wait! I must close the door----" Bang! And then came only muffled and inarticulate sound.

Down the winding stairs he sped and knelt at Allison's door. Oh, wise young daughter! not only that, but the inner, the closet door, was shut. No time for squeamishness this. Noiselessly turning the knob, he stealthily entered and tiptoed to the closet just in time to catch these words:

"Entire system will be tied up. Trainmen cannot face such assaults."

"Did you hear? Yes? They were handed Mr. Elmendorf at the door ten minutes--What? Certainly. He came in after midnight. Yes--At least I think he is--He went up to his room--Don't let him get what?--the contents? the despatches? Certainly not. Who will come for them? Why? Aren't you ever coming home? Oh, papa, do be careful! You've no idea of the wild things that--that fellow said. What? The Silver Special going out in an hour--Oh, goody!"

But Elmendorf did not stop to hear more. Slinking away, he sped down the stairway, and in another moment was hastening southward through the starlit summer night.

CHAPTER XIII.

Down in the southwestward district of the far-spreading city a howling mob of half-drunken men, women, and street-boys had surged through the freight-yards of a great railway company, and, first looting the contents, were now setting fire to the cars. Here and there along the glistening lines on which ordinarily sped the swift express or suburban trains were toppled now bulky brown boxes, with their greasy, dripping trucks protruding in air. At adjacent street-corners helmeted policemen, idly swinging their clubs behind them, looked on and laughed. Where at sundown the previous day perhaps a thousand angry-looking men and women had hovered, menacing, above the great crossing of the Central and the P.Q. & R., ten thousand furies now seemed loose. The triumphant boast of the strike-leaders that not a wheel should turn on Allison's road had been laughed to scorn. Not only had Allison, with a force of deputies and loyal trainmen, cleared his tracks at midnight and sent the famous Silver Special, full panoplied, on its way, but the armed deputies that took it to the county line brought in under cover of their Winchesters and the darkness of early morning three side-tracked trains from the far West.

And now indeed was there raging and gnashing of teeth. Men thus braved and thwarted turned to fiends. The sun was not an hour high when the emissaries of the Railway Union were haranguing the people all along these outlying districts. The striking railway-men themselves were redoubling their pleadings with the men who had stood firm, and from pleadings turned to threats. By eight o'clock the flames were shooting high from scores of cars, and under the fierce heat rails were warping and twisting. At half a dozen points the city firemen, gallant fellows, everybody's friends and defenders, loyal to their duty, had dashed up with their hose, only to be furiously assaulted and beaten back. And still the police looked on and laughed. "Like a thief in the night," screamed Elmendorf to his audience of strikers and rioters, "the P.Q. & R. has stolen its trains,--sneaked out its fell purpose. In the hours of rest and slumber, when honest men, brave men, worthy men, seek their pillows and the sanctity of their homes, these despoilers of the poor, these tyrants of a confiding people, conspiring together and corrupting with infamous gold the brethren who have betrayed us, reckless of their pledges, false to their promises--when were they ever else?--have succeeded in running two or three trains through the blockade. Now it remains with you to say how long, how great shall be their triumph. Summon from far and near your manhood and your strength. Call to action every man with a man's heart and a man's arm. See to it that none but stalwarts go on guard to-night or from this time forth, and be ready to act when the sun climbs high. Be ready, I say, for noon shall bring you tidings to make each heart bound in its seat. Be ready, a million strong if need be, to force your ultimatum down these managerial throats."

Mad with excitement and nervous strain seemed Elmendorf. From point to point his cab was dashing. He had slept but such catnaps as he could catch when whirling from one part of the city to another. It was he who rushed in to announce to the strike-leaders the astounding fact that, despite his efforts, the P. Q. & R. had pushed out the Silver Special, and was chagrined to find they knew all about it. It galled him through the night to realize that, every time he drove with tidings to anybody else, somebody was sure to be previously informed. He had left Allison's home to hasten to a point three miles distant to rouse the strikers with warnings of the proposed sending out of the train, only to find that in that as in everything else he was too late. With sympathizing spies and friends in every nook and corner, how could it be otherwise? Yet Elmendorf could never divest himself of the idea that without him to warn, advise, or control, chaos would come again. The strikers and their sympathetic mob of toughs had become dispersed during the night, and could not in time be reassembled in sufficient force to oppose successfully all those armed deputies. That was how the road was opened.

But it was closed now, and others, despite the injunctions of United States courts and the efforts of the Federal officials, found it practically useless to attempt to force even the mail trains through the rioting districts. Such was the peril to life and limb that trained engineers and firemen refused to serve, and those who dared were in some cases kicked and beaten into pulp. "Damn the United States courts!" said the mob. "Injunctions don't go here!" And so in vastly augmented numbers and in fury that vented itself in wrecking miles and miles of railway property, the mob was reopening the day. "They'll pay for last night's trick," said an official of the Railway Union, smilingly announcing another distant road tied up. "There's a higher power in the land than even the United States courts, and to-night they'll come to any terms we dictate." And he added, significantly, "Terms are already be-ing dictated."

A messenger entered at the moment. "Mr. Allison isn't at the office, and they don't know where he is. He slept awhile and breakfasted at the club, but left there half an hour ago."

"This is a matter in which probably I can be of more avail than any one else," promptly said the ubiquitous Elmendorf. "My personal acquaintance with the gen-tleman and his family may, and doubtless will, enable me to give more weight to your dictum than it might otherwise bear. Then, too, I may reasonably hope to influence him to agree to the proposed terms and render further harsh measures unnecessary."

The leaders eyed one another and hesitated. Already had they begun to see that Elmendorf assumed much more than he carried. But no one could gainsay his eagerness and devotion to the cause. Red-eyed, sleepless, pallid, he was yet here, eager to devote more hours of effort to the good cause. At all events, it would get him out of the way for a time, and he was becoming too prevalent.

"Oh, very well; if you think you can find him, Mr. Elmendorf, and obtain his written assurance that no further attempt will be made to run a train on the P.Q. & R., there's no objection. The brotherhood of Railway Trainmen stands ready and eager to back us, and if we call it out the managers are simply crushed."

And so, delighted, Elmendorf whisked away on this new mission.

Mr. Allison was not at home, such was the answer by telephone, in the silvery tones he knew so well.

"Then may I ask you to await my coming, Miss Allison?" said he. "I am charged with matters of the utmost consequence to him and to his. I will be there just as fast as a cab can carry me."

The reply was not assuring, but he went, and she waited. Indeed, the girl was waiting anxiously for her father's return. Squads of workingmen, passing the house, had shaken their fists at it and cursed its occupants. The morning wind, sweeping eastward from the lumber-yards along the North Branch, bore ominous sounds of tumult and uproar even so far from the great railway properties. Elmendorf bade his cabman wait, and rang at the bell. The tutor could let himself in with his latch-key:

the envoy of five-hundred thousand embattled freemen very properly sent his card to the magnate's daughter, and presently she appeared. Sleepless nights and sorrowing days had begun to play havoc with that fair complexion, and Florence Allison's feminine friends could not have failed to remark upon it.

But in the shrouded light of the south parlor these defects were but faintly visible. Elmendorf was pacing nervously up and down, as was his wont when deeply moved, and Miss Allison entered so quietly that he did not hear her, and became conscious of her presence on his return trip from the east window only in time to avert collision. "I beg pardon," he stammered; "I was so deep in thought. Miss Allison, permit me." And he brought forward a chair.

"Thank you, no. It can hardly take that long."

"As you will," he replied, with shrugging shoulders. "Yet I protest I deserve less arrogance of manner. Listen to me," he continued, coming impetuously towards her, whereon she coldly recoiled a pace or two. "From the heat and fury of the battle I have come here once more to attest my devotion, my loyalty, to the interests of those under whose roof I have at least found temporary shelter, if not a home and friends. I come to you clothed with power to speak and to act, turning from public duties, abandoning against their protest the control of thousands of fellow-creatures who lean on me for guidance in this crisis of their lives. On every side this morning I have heard invective, execration, denunciation, threats of the most summary vengeance hurled against your father's name. I tell you, not only does he stand in peril of his life, but that this household, even you--you, so fair, so gentle, so delicate--may at any moment become the prey of a populace as frenzied as ever dragged to the guillotine the shrieking beauties of the Court of France. Miss Allison, whatsoever may be the injustice with which your father has treated me, it sinks into nothingness in comparison with my sense of the peril that threatens you. I am charged with a mission of most sacred character. I am the envoy of the masses, sent to present their last plea to the man. You know where he is: my carriage is at the door: as you would save him and save yourself, I adjure you to accompany me at once and add your prayers to mine to bend his obdurate heart. Nay, Florence, I implore----"

But Miss Allison had darted back, a fine flush mounting to her forehead at the climax of his impassioned address. She had faint appreciation of histrionics.

"Mr. Elmendorf, I think you're simply crazy," was her eminently practical way of putting an end to the address. "If you wish to see pa--my father, you'll find him at the managers' office at half-past ten, or if you hurry you may catch him at the Lambert." And then she would have turned; but he sprang to her.

"How can you treat me with disdain?" he said. "Because I have been poor, is that reason why I may not one day be rolling in wealth? Number you among your friends my superior in education, in intellect? Is it in the ranks of these empty-headed officers or these brainless, vapid sons of vice and luxury that make up the men of your social circle, you are to be mated? I tell you that this movement means revolution, that within this very week the long-oppressed people shall be paramount, and we who reap shall rule. I have long seen it coming, long foretold and long been ridiculed, but now the hour, ay, the hour and the man have come. Already I have saved you from the dishonor of alliance with---- Nay, you must listen," for, with infinite disgust upon her face, she turned angrily away. But, as she would not listen, he sprang forward and seized her wrists. "Florence," he cried, "I----"

And then her voice re-echoed through the hall. "Cary!" she screamed, and far aloft there was a shout of "Coming!" and, six steps at a bound, that exuberant specimen of Young America came thundering down the broad spiral of the stairway. The portentous butler, too, hove suddenly in sight. Elmendorf dropped the subject--and her wrist, whisked his hat off the hall table, and was out of the house and into his cab before the wrathful brother could reach him.

Not until cabby had driven blindly for six blocks did Elmendorf poke his cane through the trap and bid him speed for the Lambert. A carriage stood at the private entrance, and the driver said it was Mr. Allison's. The anteroom was open; the glazed doors to the private office were closed, but excited voices arose from within. He recognized Allison's, Wells's, and that of the chairman of the board of trustees, in hot altercation. The chairman seemed siding with Wells, which added to Allison's wrath, and he wound up with an explosion:

"I've given you more than reason enough. She has been shut up here alone with him time and again at night; she has been seen going to his rooms long after dark; she has been seen walking or driving with him as late as midnight; and the very evening he is due at a gentleman's house at dinner he sends 'urgent business' as his plea, and is found supping alone with her at the Belmont. If she stays, I resign."

"And I answer," thundered Wells, "that that girl's as pure-hearted a woman as ever lived. She has been shut up here with me time and again, working at my letters until late at night; she has been to my rooms a dozen times to leave her finished work on her homeward way; she has been seen, or could have been seen, walking or driving with me late at night, for I'm proud to say I've taken her home instead of letting her go it alone in the rain; and as for the Belmont, it's the nearest and neatest restaurant I know of, and a dozen times when we had work to be finished in a hurry have I taken her, as Mr. Forrest did, to have her cup of tea there, instead of letting her tramp two miles to get it at home. I'm a married man, and he isn't; that's the only difference. You say if she stays, you resign. All right, Mr. Allison. If she goes, I go."

And then upon this stormy scene entered Elmendorf, the blessed, the peacemaker.

"It would be idle to assume ignorance of the subject of this conference," he began, before any one had sufficiently recovered from surprise to head him off, "and, as it is audible throughout this portion of the building, I could not but hear and be attracted by it. I am here, as ever, to take the side of the oppressed, and to say that should that young woman be punished thus summarily for her--indiscretions, I shall consider it my duty to make public certain circumstances in connection with the case, notably Mr. Forrest's relations with certain families in our midst, that may prove unpleasant reading."

"Enough of this, Mr. Elmendorf," began Wells, angrily. "This young woman, as you term her, is not to be summarily punished, because she has done nothing to deserve it, and despite every sneaking endeavor on your part to cloud her good name. And now, like the double-dealing cad you are, you come here posing as her defender. She needs none, by God, as long as my wife and I are left in the land; and I would trust her cause with Mr. Allison himself at any other time than now, when he is overstrained and worn out.--Miss Wallen is at home," he continued, addressing himself to the two trustees, "owing, she explains, to her mother's severe illness. She, too, is far from well. She has been looking badly for weeks. I was going up there to see what I could do for her, when surprised by this visit. Mr. Waldo, as president of the board of trustees you may understand that I declare these allegations against Miss Wallen to be utterly, brutally unjust, and that I protest against the action proposed by Mr. Allison. Most unfortunately our talk has been overheard by the man whom of all others I distrust in this connection."

"What business have you here, Mr. Elmendorf, anyway?" said Allison, glowering angrily. "I have forbidden you my doors, yet you follow me."

"My business is with you, sir, not as a suppliant pleading for mercy, as you seem to think, but as the representative of a great people demanding immediate answer to their----"

"What? Why, you meddling, insignificant----" scowled Allison, gripping his cane as though eager to use it.

"Spare your insults and your cane, Mr. Allison. Our relative positions have been utterly reversed in the last forty-eight hours. At this moment there is a clamor for your downfall in the throats of three hundred thousand toil-worn, honest laboring men. Between their victim and their vengeance no State, no municipal authority will interpose a hand. Last night, false to your promises to the Brotherhood of Trainmen, you sent strong bodies of armed men to terrorize the few strikers gathered in the effort to establish their just claims. You broke their blockade, ran your trains in and out, and indulged in insolent triumph before the people in the morning press. At this moment within easy range of your palatial home ten thousand determined men are assembled, awaiting the word. Once launched upon their work, not one stone of your railway buildings, not a shingle on the roofs of your elevators, not one brick in the walls of your homestead, will be left to show where once they stood. Only my appeals, only my urgent counsels, have thus far restrained them. What will be the consequences if you refuse to listen God alone can tell. Despite my personal wrongs, I have come to you as mediator, deprecating riots and destruction. All the Union asks of you, all I implore you to do is to sign a written promise that until such time as this unhappy controversy be settled the railway company of which you are the virtual head will make no further attempt to move a single train."

Allison's face was a sight to see, purpling with wrath and amaze, yet quivering with sense of the wild absurdity of the situation. Glancing from one to another, portly Mr. Waldo stood uneasily by. He believed some escaped lunatic had invaded the Lambert. Even Wells, who had known Elmendorf for months, seemed unprepared for the sublimity of this flight. He turned away towards the window to let them settle it between them. At last Allison spoke, with exaggerated calm:

"And if I refuse this modest request, what am I to expect as the consequence?"

"The immediate consequence will be the calling out at noon to-day of the Brotherhood of Railway Trainmen and the Brotherhood of Locomotive Engineers, thus tying up every road in the country, to be followed to-morrow by similar action on the part of the Knights of Labor, involving every industry in the land and turning millions of idle men loose upon our streets. What will stand between you, your hoarded wealth, and your cherished ones--your lives--and the wild vengeance of a long oppressed and starving populace, I leave you to imagine."

"And you actually expect me to believe this trash,--expect me to believe that the State of Illinois will stand idly by and see----"

"The governor of Illinois," interrupted Elmendorf, "has refused to interfere. His heart beats in sympathy with that of his people. He knows their wrongs. He has dared to say that never by his call shall sabre or bayonet be used to intimidate the workingman in the effort to secure his rights. The blood of the martyred men you hanged eight years ago as Anarchists cries aloud for vengeance, and the day of the people has come at last. They govern the governor; *they* are the legislature of Illinois, and when they rise no power on earth can save you."

But Wells could stand it no longer. He was fuming at the great window overlooking the street, and now burst impetuously into speech. "No power on earth, you absurd lunatic? do you mean that because this State has a crank like you temporarily at the top there's nothing beyond or behind it to save us from pillage and murder and anarchy? Listen to that, you foreign-born fraud!" and far up the street the morning air was ringing with shouts of acclaim; "listen to that! There's some American music for you, you half-witted, stall-fed socialist!" For loud and clear a trumpet-call echoed down the thoroughfare. "Look at that!" he cried, throwing aside the lower shutters, "look at that, you mad-brained, moon-blinded dreamer!"

And there, covering the space almost from curb to curb, a squadron of regular cavalry came sweeping down the avenue, the guidons fluttering over the uniforms of dusty blue, the drab campaign hats shading the stern, soldierly faces, the grim cartridge-belts bulging with copper and lead, the ugly little brown barkers of carbines and revolvers peeping from their holsters. Troop after troop, they swung steadily by, the guns of a light battery following close at their heels. "No power on earth!" persisted the incensed man of books. "You stuffed owl! Go back to your mobs and murderers, and when you've told them what you've seen, keep going until you get back out of this to the country where such as you belong,--if there is one on earth that'll own you,--and tell them the United States is a government, a *Nation*,--by the Eternal! and don't you dare forget it again." And, stupefied, thunderstruck, Elmendorf turned and fled.

"But this is invasion! this is treason!" he gasped, as he bolted madly from the room.

CHAPTER XIV.

And these were but the advanced guard of the little army of regulars that, welcomed with glad acclaim by every law-abiding, order-loving citizen, came pouring into Chicago all through that day and for some days that followed, their very presence bringing assurance of peace and safety to thousands and thousands of anxious householders, and confusion and dismay to the leaders of the mob. Believing as had these latter that, despite the vast and valuable Federal properties in the heart of the city, despite the fact that some of the railways involved were at that very moment under the wing of the Federal courts, despite the laws of the general government affecting the working and management of every one of over a dozen great trunk lines centring in Chicago, Uncle Sam would be ass enough to confide them all to the care of State authorities notoriously dependent upon the masses, and that he would not venture to protect his property, sustain his courts, enforce his laws, demand and command respect and subordination, or even venture upon his own, except at the invitation and permission of a hesitant State government, there had been little short of triumph and exultation in the camp of the American Railway Union until this fatal July morning. Now their wrath was frantic.

And Elmendorf was madder than ever. The general and his staff reappeared in the midst of the concentration. Their coming was announced. After vainly haranguing the stolid officials at head-quarters upon the enormity of their conduct in declining to see the fearful blunder made by their President and commander-in-chief, after attempting to harangue a battalion of dusty infantry in the vague hope that, inspired by his eloquence, they might do something the enlisted men of the

United States never yet have done, no matter what the temptation,--revolt against their government and join the army of the new revolution,--and being induced to desist only when summarily told to "Go on out of that! or----" while a bayonet supplied the ellipsis, poor Elmendorf flew to the station, to be the first to meet the general on his return and to open his eyes to a proper conception of law, order, and soldierly duty. Even here those minions from head-quarters were ahead of him. Three or four officers were already on the spot awaiting their chief, and Elmendorf felt convinced that they had come solely to prevent his getting the ear of the commander. Even as they waited and a curious crowd began to gather, numbers of strike sympathizers among them, down the broad steps from the street above came the tramp, tramp of martial feet, and in solid column of fours, in full marching order, every man a walking arsenal of ball cartridges, a battalion of infantry filed sturdily into the grimy train-shed, formed line, facing the murmuring crowd, and then stood there in composed silence "at ease." Then the little knot of staff-officers and newspaper men was presently joined by Lieutenant-Colonel Kenyon, commanding the --th Infantry, one battalion of which had just taken position as indicated; and to him came others, officers of the battalion. Again did Elmendorf raise his voice in appeal for the rights of his fellow-men.

"Colonel Kenyon," he declaimed, his shrill tones distinctly audible above the hoarse murmur of voices in the rapidly augmenting throng, "you have been so considerate as to listen to a humble outsider before this, and to express appreciation of some, at least, of the views I have felt constrained to express. You are, as I understand, the commanding officer of the regiment that has just arrived in this city. You are an officer sworn to maintain the Constitution of the United States; and is not your very presence here--you and your men--in glaring violation of that Constitution?"

Here the few officers who had joined their commander, all strangers to Elmendorf, turned upon him in astonishment. The newspaper men chuckled and nudged each other companionably. Some of the staff turned away, plainly indicating that they had already had to listen to too much of that sort of thing. Kenyon looked him curiously over.

"Mr. Elmendorf, do you ask that question in your sober senses, or only as a jocular reminder? Those identical words were addressed to me by an irate gentleman in Virginia in '62." So far from being irritated, old Kenyon seemed to find amusement in drawing his interlocutor out.

"Ah, but, my dear sir, there the whole State--the whole South--was in armed rebellion against the Federal government. Here is neither insurrection nor rebellion. Here, honest, law-abiding, patriotic men, as loyal to the Union of States as ever you could be, are exerting their prerogative as men, their rights as citizens, to obtain justice for themselves and their brethren at the hands of a defiant and oppressive monopoly. They have done no wrong, violated no law, and yet here you come with bayonets and ball cartridges to intimidate, if not to shoot down in cold blood, husbands and fathers and peaceable citizens who are only pleading for justice at the hands of their employers."

"Some mistake here, Mr. Elmendorf. Your leaders have already declared it a rebellion. The husbands and fathers we are here to look after are the amiable parties who stove in our car-windows and soaped our rails and let drive such pygmy projectiles as coupling-pins, a wild switch engine or two, and blazing freight-cars at us as we came in awhile ago."

"Our people are in no wise connected with that," cried Elmendorf. "All this alleged violence is the work of lawless classes whom we cannot control, or of the emissaries of the railways themselves. It has been grossly and purposely exaggerated."

"Oh! Then all this rioting is done by outsiders, not by your friends the strikers, who heartily condemn the whole business, do they?"

"Most assuredly. We have forbidden violence in any and every form."

"I see. And yet the rabble and the railway folks have insisted on it. Well, now, how grateful you ought to be to the President for ordering us here to help you suppress them! Really, Mr. Elmendorf, I am glad to find we are on the same side of this question, after all." But here a shout of laughter drowned Kenyon's words and drove Elmendorf frantic.

"You don't understand," he almost shrieked. "It is our people who are intimidated,--beaten back in the moment of victory." And then some of the crowd, now thronging the open space in front of the battalion, began to cheer. A man pushed through, handed Kenyon a telegram, and whispered a few words in his ear. Kenyon glanced quickly around upon the multitude now surging close about the group, and stepped back a few paces to read his despatch. Elmendorf followed, eager to resume his harangue. Kenyon uplifted his hand. "Pardon me now, Mr. Elmendorf. I have business to attend to." But Elmendorf was wild with excitement and wrath. He had been laughed at,--he, the mover of millions. Here were already a thousand fellow-citizens at his back, and more coming. From the freight-yards up and down the tracks, from the docks, the elevators, the neighboring saloons, they were swarming to the scene. There in double rank stood the four compact little companies of regulars in the business-like rig of blue and brown, resting on their arms, chatting in low tones, or calmly surveying from under the broad hat-brims the gathering crowd. To their right and left, up and down the long vista of train-sheds, letting themselves down from overarching bridges, or pushing boldly past the feeble railway police, hundreds of tough-looking citizens were slowly closing in. Back of the battalion, separated from it by only two tracks, were long files of passenger and Pullman cars, behind which and on whose platforms, in knots of half a dozen, other men were gathering. It was the general superintendent of the road who had spoken to Kenyon and was now exchanging a few words with the chief quartermaster of the department. Dozens in the crowd pushed forward instantly, newspaper men as a matter of business, others from curiosity, as Kenyon opened his despatch. A burly, gray-haired major was quickly at his side, and a tall young sub-altern, the adjutant of the regiment. One brief glance over the paper, and the commander turned to his right. "Clear the station," was all he said. Major Cross touched his hat, an eager light shooting across his frank, soldierly face, and strode quickly back to the line. A mere gesture brought the four company commanders to him. Not a dozen words were spoken, but in an instant the swords of the officers leaped from their scabbards, and then, obeying some low-toned commands, the right and left flank companies, simply lifting their rifle-butts, enough to clear the ground, changed front to right and left respectively, thus bringing them facing the outer ends of the train-sheds. About a dozen men, led by a sergeant, broke suddenly away from the eastward flank of each of the two companies thus moved, and, without so much as an audible word, scattered away to the passenger-cars, covering a hundred yards of their length in a dozen seconds. Then under the cars dove some of the lot, up the steps sprang others, and away before them scattered the intruders. A long brick wall hemmed the yards in at the eastern side, and there, dividing into two parties in the same prompt, business-like way, the squads drove before them north

or south every one of the late lookers-on, some grinning, some scowling and swear-
ing, some remonstrating, but all going. Up from the throats of the dense throng in
front of the battalion went a chorus of jeers and laughter. It is always fun to one part
of a street crowd to see some other part of it, especially if it occupied a better point
of view, driven from its enviable ground. The moment the space behind their new
alignment was thus cleared, the flank companies each threw forward another squad
of eight, which, promptly shaking itself out into a long thin rank and fixing bayonet
as it went, marched straight at the thin crowds which had entered the station along
the right of way. A solid platoon followed in support, and in less time than it takes
to tell it the populace was on the move.

Then came the turn of the centre companies; and here a very different problem
presented itself. Leading up to the street was one broad stairway in the middle of the
great depot building, and one, somewhat narrower, a hundred feet farther north,
next to the baggage-rooms. Between the tracks and the offices on this floor, enclos-
ing a space perhaps a hundred yards in length by ten in breadth, was a high iron
fence, pierced here and there with little turnstile gates, now closed, and by three
or four rolling gates, the main or centre one of which stood open. This was directly
opposite the broad stairway. It was this through which the battalion had marched,
the newspaper men and officials had followed, and the crowd had speedily bulged.
No good would result from shoving back this protruding swarm of curious or com-
bative citizens, for the space behind the bars was packed solid. The crowd began
to grin and exchange jocular remarks. It would take a long time to squeeze them
back through the stairway, and meanwhile they could have lots of fun, and Elmendorf a chance for a speech, so they began to shout for him. He was still squeaking
and gesticulating about the knot of newspaper men and staff-officers, but Kenyon,
climbing on a baggage-truck, was calmly looking over the sea of upturned and often
leeringly impudent faces beyond the grating. Then he called Major Cross to his side,
and together they looked it over.

The crowd began to wax facetious. They knew the soldiers wouldn't shoot so
long as they were not shooting. They knew they wouldn't prod with their bayonets
men who manifestly couldn't get back. They thought they had the regulars, in fine,
where they couldn't do a blessed thing unless the police would come and pull the
crowd out from behind, and the police were not interfering with the populace just

then. An American street crowd is gifted with a fine sense of humor, and the sight of these two veteran officers perched on a baggage-truck and reconnoitring their ground was full of suggestion. "Don't jump on us, major: we couldn't stand them feet!" shouted one jovial tough. "A speech from Old-Man-Afraid-Of-His-Dignity!" sang out a second. The gang guffawed, and the officers went on with their conference utterly unmoved, deaf, apparently, to the salutations. Then Kenyon climbed down and said a word to the superintendent, who nodded appreciatively. The adjutant went one way, the regimental quartermaster the other. Each took half a dozen men from the supporting platoons of the flank companies, who had by this time pushed the scattering throng beyond the yard limits and set their guards at the entrances. Then the gray-headed, white-moustached major whipped out his watch and held up his hand. There was a good deal of chaff going on, but a half-silence fell on the throng.

"All that space in there will be needed in five minutes from this time," he said, in a quiet, conversational tone. "The way out is open, and you will oblige me very much by quietly withdrawing. Begin the move back there by the main staircase, and up there also, if you please, so that these gentlemen who are crowded in here can follow you. Move at once, and you'll be out in plenty of time."

Not a few on the outskirts did begin subordinately to move away, and a dozen or more were already going up the steps, when the crowd gave tongue. "Come back, there. Stay where you are. We've got as much right here as they have," were the cries. And then the luckless Elmendorf was seized with an inspiration. Bounding upon a baggage-truck, he waved his hat and shouted, "Hear me, fellow-citizens. You have said right. We have indeed more right here than these----" But here a muscular hand grasped him by the seat of his trousers, and Elmendorf's speech wound up in a shriek, as he was lifted backward off the truck, a big Irish sergeant glowering at him as he landed him on *terra firma*. "I yield to force," screamed Elmendorf. "Go and tell it." And then between a couple of brawny, unsympathetic soldiers he was rushed back, and, in the twinkling of an eye, hustled into the smoking-compartment of a vacant Pullman and there locked in, with a bayonet at the window. For a moment the throng howled, but there was no forward impulse. The motionless line of the two centre companies seemed to have a soothing effect, and still the major coolly stood there, watch in hand. Two minutes passed, three, and not ten men of the crowd had slipped away. Certain railway men and reporters edged forward, away from the crowd. Certain of the crowd strove to follow, but some men in plain clothing whipped open their coats, displaying silver stars, and warned them back. Three minutes and a half, and still the major stood calmly glancing over the crowd and then at his watch, and then the corners of his mouth began to twitch, for he had cast one quick glance up and down the line of that iron fence. Unreeling something behind them as they reappeared, the squads that had followed the regimental staff officers quickly trotted into sight again at the upper and lower ends of the pen, and the outskirts of the crowd "caught on" at a glance. They were manning the hose. Already the gleaming nozzles were being screwed on, and the humor of the situation became suddenly clouded. "Watch out!" was the cry from both ends of the dense mass. Dozens of men at the north end who could readily escape were already in rush for the upper stairway, but those at the south were less lucky. A dense mass of fellow-citizens was wedged between them and the exits, but rapidly the alarm was spreading inward from the flanks. "Four minutes," said the major, grimly, though his lips were twitching like mad. Then the upturned faces began to blanch, the crowd to heave and swell, and a backward sway sent a hundred or more surging up the main staircase. The next minute panic seemed to seize on all, for the jeers gave way to shouts of fright and pain as men were squeezed breathless in the crush; and then, tumbling over one another's heels, climbing one another's backs in sheep-like terror, they fought for air and escape, and the last coat-tails went streaming up the stairs sharp on time, as Kenyon said, with the bayonets of the left centre company threateningly close in their wake.

Once out in the open street, they strove to rally and encourage one another and to shower defiance and stones at their assailants; but these latter contented themselves with clearing a space for carriages about the doors and calmly stationing their guards to hold it; and when, a few moments later, the general's special train came steaming in, Elmendorf raged in vain. There was neither orator nor deputation to meet him on behalf of the strike-leaders. Not until after the chief had driven away in his carriage was the agitator released from the hated confines of the Pullman and bidden to go his way. Fuming with the indignity of his position, he left, vowing that he would return if there was law in the land, backed with warrants for the arrest of Kenyon for felonious assault and false imprisonment; and Kenyon smiled and said the warrant wouldn't surprise him in the least.

And then followed the stirring scenes of a riot week that showed not only the depth and extent of the insurrectionary spirit among the unlettered masses of the people, but also the wisdom of the President in ordering the prompt concentration of regular troops in the heart of the threatened city. Silently, in disciplined order, the various detachments had marched to their stations. Silently, in disciplined order, puny in points of numbers as compared with the vast mob of their howling antagonists, they faced the throng, grimly peering from under their slouched hat-brims, gripping with their brown, sinewy hands the muzzles of the old trusty rifles, listening with utter amaze, with tingling nerves, to the furious yells of "Down with the government!" "To hell with the United States!" and wondering how long their fathers would have stood such treason thirty years ago. Calm, grim, and silent, conscious of their power, merciful in their strength, superb in their disdain of insult, their contempt of danger, their indifference to absolute outrage,--for maddened men showered the ranks with mud and gravel, and foul-mouthed, slatternly women--vile, unclean harpies of the slums--dipped their brooms in the reeking gutters and slashed their filth into the stern, soldierly faces,--for hours, for days, they coolly held that misguided, drink-crazed, demagogue-excited mob at bay, reopening railways, protecting trains, escorting Federal officials, forcing passage after passage through the turbulent districts, until the fury of the populace wore itself out against the rock of their iron discipline, and one after another the last of the rioters slunk to their holes, unharmed by even one avenging shot. Fire and flame had wrought their havoc, miles of railway lines and cars had been wrecked and ruined, but otherwise the mad-brained effort had utterly failed of its purpose, and for the third time had the regulars stood almost the sole bulwark between the great city and absolute anarchy. True, the regiments of the National Guard were at last ordered into service, but not until after the presence of the Federal force had given assurance that, whether the State officials liked it or not, the general government would tolerate such insurrection no longer. True, the State troops stood ready, eager to do their work, and some of them, at least, so capable, so drilled and disciplined, that, left to the orders of their own officers, they could and would have suppressed the riots. But, there was the difference, even when called into action the most reliable and experienced of the regimental commanders were practically deprived of their commands; their regiments were broken up into pygmy detachments and scattered hither and thither by companies and squads, covering sometimes a tract of suburbs fifteen miles long and half as wide, while the entire force was placed under the orders of a city official notoriously in sympathy with the initial strike and seeking the suffrages of the very class from which the mobs were drawn. The extraordinary spectacle was seen of a veteran colonel with only half a company to guard the head-quarters of the regiment in a remote and dangerous spot, and absolutely forbidden to summon any of his own regiment to his defence in case of emergency, except upon the advice and consent of some official of the city police. Well was it for Chicago and the nation that the President of the United States stood as unmoved by the puerile protests of the demagogue in office as were his loyal soldiery by the fury of insult, abuse, and violence heaped upon them by that mob of demagogue-supporters.

"By heaven," said the editor of a great daily to old Kenyon at the close of the week, "I never dreamed of such superb discipline, and under such foul insult. I swear I don't see how you fellows could stand it."

"Oh," said Kenyon, grimly, "it wasn't half as hard to bear as what your columns have been saying about us any time these last five years."

CHAPTER XV.

When the President of the United States declined to withdraw the regulars from Chicago as urged by the governor of Illinois, Mr. Elmendorf decided that it was because he had not been heard from on the subject, and so started for Washington. This was how it happened that he abandoned his project of leading his friends and fellow-citizens in their determined assault upon the serried ranks of capital, backed though they were by "the bristling bayonets of a usurper." For several days his deluded disciples looked for him in vain. The telegraphic despatches of the Associated Press told briefly of another crank demanding audience at the White House, claiming to represent the people of Chicago and persisting in his demand until, "yielding to force," he was finally ejected. But Elmendorf was silent upon this episode when he returned, so the story could hardly have referred to him. Calling at Allison's to attend to the long-deferred duty of packing his trunk, he was informed by the butler that that labor had been spared him and that he would find all his things at his former lodging-place, Mrs. Wallen's. Going thither to claim them, he was met at the threshold by Mart, whose face was gaunt and white and worn, and who no sooner caught sight of the once revered features of the would-be labor leader than he fell upon them with his fists and fragmentary malediction. Mart battered and thumped, while Elmendorf backed and protested. It was a policeman, one of that body whom ever since '86 Elmendorf had loved to designate as "bloodhounds of the rich man's laws," who lifted Mart off his prostrate victim, and Mrs. McGrath who partially raised the victim to his feet. No sooner, however, had she recognized him than she loosed her hold, flopped him back into the gutter, and, addressing the policeman, bade him "Fur the love of hivvin set him on again!" which the policeman declined to do, despite Mrs. McGrath's magnificent and descriptive denunciation, addressed to the entire neighborhood, in which Elmendorf's personal character and professional career came in for glowing and not altogether inaccurate portrayal. Slowly the dishevelled scholar found his legs, Mart making one more effort to break away from the grasp of the law and renew the attack before he was led to the station-house, where, however, he had not long to languish before a major of cavalry rode up and bailed him out; but by that time, and without his luggage, the victim of his wrath had disappeared. "There's three weeks' board ag'in' it," said Mrs. McGrath, "and the ould lady not buried three days, and the young lady sick and cryin' her purty eyes out, and divil a cint or sup in the house for Mart's wife and babies, barrin' what me and Mac could spare 'em. Och, that's only wan of five-and-twinty families that furrin loonattic has ruined."

At the camp of his squadron Major Cranston had been informed by his veteran, McGrath, of the reappearance of Elmendorf, and of the arrest of Mart for spoiling his beauty. Mac also told something of the straits to which Mart's family were reduced. Mrs. Mac had known Mrs. Mart in the days when, as a blooming school-girl, the latter used to trip by the Cranston homestead, and had striven to aid her through the failing fortunes of the months preceding Mart's last strike; it was her voluble account of the state of affairs that prompted this soft-hearted squadron commander to take Mart by the hand and bid him tell his troubles. Mart broke down. He'd been a fool and a dupe, he knew and realized it, but Elmendorf had so preached about his higher destiny and the absolute certainty of triumph and victory if they but made one grand concerted effort, that he had staked all on the result, and lost it. He knew it was all up with the strikers when once the general government said stop, and so had gone home, to be greeted by the tidings that his mother was sick unto death. Jenny was there, calm, brave, silent, full of resource, but, oh, so pale and wan! She had employed the best physician to be had, but she alone would be nurse. She never reproached, never chided him for his long absence when most needed. Then had followed a few days of sorrow and suspense, and then the gentle, harmless, helpless, purposeless life fluttered away. Jenny paid all the bills, the doctor, the undertaker, everything, and Mart tried vainly to get some work; but he was a marked man. Then, the day after Jenny had settled up everything and made herself some simple mourning garb, she went to resume her duties at the library, and came back in a little while, white and ill, and she had been very ill since,--out of her head at times, he believed, said Mart, and he had gone and got the doctor whom she had employed for her mother, a kind fellow who had been unremitting in his attentions, and who told him bluntly to shut up when he talked about not knowing where the money was to come from to pay him, and said that that little woman was worth ten times her weight in gold, which, said Mart, was God's truth, as he himself ought to have had sense enough to know before.

Little by little, as they walked homeward together, Cranston's orderly riding with the horses along the street, and dozens of people turning curiously to gaze at the cavalry officer and the late striker, it began to dawn upon Cranston that Mart's sister, who was worth so much more than her weight in gold, was the very Miss Wallen who had been so oddly unwilling to write at his dictation the letter to El-mendorf. Arrived at the house, he was sure of it, for there, with solemn face, was Mr. Wells. "My wife," said he, "is up-stairs, trying to see what she can do. This is Martin Wallen, is it?--Well, Martin, I regret exceedingly to hear you assaulted Mr. Elmendorf to-day--and didn't kill him."

Manifestly Mr. Wells was not a proper person for the position he held, being far too impulsive in speech for a bookish man; but then Wells had been sorely tried. He told Cranston something of it as they walked away together after loading Mart with provisions and fruit at the corner grocery. Together they stopped to see Dr. Francis and have a brief chat with him about his patient, and then Cranston mounted and rode thoughtfully back to camp at the lake front. Captain Davies, with his troop, had just returned from a long day's dusty, dirty, exasperating duty at the stock-yards, and no sooner had he made his brief report than the major queried, "Do you happen to know whether Forrest is back with his regiment?"

"He was commanding his company at the yards to-day, sir. I heard he returned four days ago."

"H'm!" said the major, reflectively: "I think I'll stroll over to-night and find Kenyon."

They were both sons of Chicago, these two field officers, and had always been close friends. Forrest, however, was a New Yorker, many years their junior in the service. Cranston had liked him well, yet now he felt that he should be glad to consult Kenyon, who had known him still longer, for that which he had heard from Wells as they walked to the doctor's filled him with vague anxiety. In common with most society people, Cranston shared the belief that, if not actually engaged to Florence Allison, Forrest certainly would be as soon as old Allison's objections were removed; but in speaking of the probable cause of Miss Wallen's illness Wells had used some vehement language. Plainly the librarian told Cranston of the stormy interview between Allison and himself, in which, in presence of Mr. Waldo and "that man Elmendorf," Allison had demanded her discharge. Plainly he told him his own views of Miss Wallen's character and conduct, and what his wife thought of her,-- that she was a girl to be honored and admired and respected above her kind; "but," said he, "Mr. Forrest always treated her as though he thought so too, and it may be that she learned to care for him before she had heard about his being a suitor for the hand of Miss Allison. I sent the girl who was temporarily occupying her place back into the library when we had our talk," said Wells, "but I reckon she didn't go beyond the passage-way and heard pretty much the whole thing. Allison bellowed, like the bull he is, and perhaps I did, too. Still, it hadn't occurred to me to question her on the subject, though I was minded to tell her if she had heard anything she was on no account to repeat it or any part of it; but Miss Wallen came back to her desk sooner than I expected, and the moment this young minx hesitatingly told me she had been here and had gone home I suspected something, and presently pumped the whole truth out of her. The contemptible meanness of some women passes all my descriptive powers. There are several girls employed in the library, and it seems some of them were jealous of Miss Wallen, or rather of her superior position, and one evening that fellow Elmendorf got in there and threatened her with exposure or something of the kind and insulted her, so that she slapped his face, and two of those library girls heard it. It happened just before Forrest came in, and he found her all quivering and unstrung. She was to have finished some work for him that evening, and he was to have dined at Allison's, but she was so broken up it was some time before she could go on with it. Neither could she tell him the cause. Well, it was one of these very girls whom, all unthinkingly, I had put in her place, and what does the little wretch do the morning that Jeannette returned but tell her all about Allison's row with me, and his demand and reasons for her discharge! Of course she didn't tell of my refusal; she says she didn't happen to hear that, which is a lie, I reckon. However, that's the big, big last pound that broke the heart of that poor hard-working, long-suffering girl and sent her home a sick woman. Francis says she'll pull through; but what do you suppose will come of it even then?" Wells told him more about poor Jenny, all the story of her long, brave struggle so far as he knew it, which was far less than the facts, and Cranston wished with all his heart that Meg, his own bonny wife, were home to help and counsel. All the same he meant to see Kenyon, and later, perhaps, Forrest.

But he saw the latter first.

There was a brilliant gathering at the club that night. Matters had so quieted down in the disturbed districts that many of the regular officers had been permitted to accept invitations to be present. Allison had not wished to go, but Florence begged. She was looking "absolutely saffron," said Aunt Lawrence, and if something wasn't done to break up that child's nervous melancholy she wouldn't be responsible for her. That she herself was in the faintest degree responsible for the alleged nervous melancholy Aunt Lawrence would not have admitted for a moment. Allison was in evil humor, as is many a better man when beginning to realize that he has made an ass of himself. Wells had been after him with a hot stick on discovering that the only authority for his accusations against Miss Wallen was "that devil's tool Elmendorf and a creature of his own coaching." Allison knew, moreover, that Forrest was back, commanding a company of his regiment, for his own associates were pouring into his ears their praises for Forrest's nerve and calm courage in facing with only twenty men a furious mob of nearly a thousand and rescuing some so-called "scabs" from their hands, poor fellows who had been pulled from the platforms of the P.Q. & R. trains. "He's 'way down below the stock-yards, anyhow, and won't be there to-night," said Allison to himself: so, at ten o'clock, with Florence on his arm, he entered the brilliantly lighted parlor. It was full of well-gowned women and of men in the appropriate garb of the hour and occasion, while not a few of the officers were in uniform. The general and some of his staff were almost the first to greet them. Presently Mr. Sloan joined the party, and the first thing he did was to begin telling of Forrest's prediction as to the attitude of the general government in the event of trouble. Allison shifted uncomfortably, the general and his aides looked politely interested, and somebody attempted to make some arch remark for Miss Allison's ears, but she was plainly nervous and ill at ease. The chief presently presumed Miss Florence had heard how admirably Forrest had behaved in the rescue of certain railway men from the mob the previous day, and Florence owned that she had heard nothing at all,--it was the first intimation she had that Forrest was there; whereat the three officers looked astonished and embarrassed. Evidently something was amiss. There had perhaps been a quarrel. "Oh," said Captain Morris, in prompt explanation, "Forrest was away down in the depths of Oklahoma when he heard his regiment was ordered here, and he had to wait for telegraphic authority to come on. He never even got up into town. His company was at Grand Crossing, and he joined it there. He hasn't been north of the stock-yards since."

But Allison got away as quickly as possible. This sort of thing wasn't helping Flo to forget, and presently Flo herself concluded she'd rather go home, and just at eleven o'clock they came forth to their carriage. Three officers in full uniform were directly in front, chatting with two others in rough campaign rig, and the taller, slenderer of these latter, a soldierly, brown-eyed fellow with a heavy moustache and a week-old brown stubble on cheeks and chin, stepped quickly forward and whipped off his drab slouch hat. For the first time in her life Florence Allison saw her friend the lieutenant in service dress, and knew not what to say. All the response to his cordial "Good-evening, Miss Allison. How are you, Mr. Allison?" was the hurried hustling past of the pair, the girl with averted head, the father reddening and embarrassed. Florence was bundled quickly into the carriage, and then Allison turned. "You'll have to excuse my daughter to-night, Mr. Forrest. She isn't well, and--er--er--I'll hope to see you to-morrow." And, lifting his hat, he followed Florence. The door was slammed, and away they went, leaving Forrest gazing after them in no pleasant frame of mind.

Major Cranston touched his arm. "Come over to my tent, Forrest. I can explain something of this," he said.

And the next morning, after some sleepless hours, with permission from Colonel Kenyon to be absent from camp until noon, Mr. Forrest took a cab and drove far up town, making only one stop--at a florist's--on the way. The Allison carriage was coming forth just as he reached the well-known gates. Mrs. Lawrence and Florence, seated therein, did not catch sight of the occupant of the cab until he raised his hat. Florence gasped, grabbed Aunt Lawrence by the arm, called to their coachman, and glanced back.

But no, Mr. Forrest had no thought of stopping there at all. The cab drove straight on past the Allison homestead, and something told her whither it was bound.

CHAPTER XVI.

Mr. Allison did not meet Lieutenant Forrest that day as he had "hoped to." He did not hope to at all. He hoped not to for several days, and a very uncomfortable man he was. Forrest, however, seemed making no effort to find him, as the millionaire rather expected him to do. Forrest's duties were somewhat confining, and Allison even kept away from his pet club awhile, dreading to meet with officers who were being entertained there at all hours. The Lambert was another place that for a while he religiously avoided. He was becoming afraid of Wells. It gave him a queer feeling, however, when driving home to luncheon one day, to see an orderly holding two officers' horses opposite the private entrance, and Cranston and Forrest in conversation with Mr. Wells. They were absorbed and did not look up, but something told Allison there was trouble ahead for him. Even his friend Waldo had been embarrassed and constrained in his presence. He made up his mind to stop and see Wells that very afternoon, and did so, bursting in in his fine old English manner. After fidgeting a few moments until Wells had had his stenographer (acting) withdraw, he impetuously began:

"Hum--haw--Wells, tell me about that girl. How's she getting on?"

"If by 'that girl,' Allison, you mean Miss Wallen, she's not getting on at all. A lady who is robbed of her mother, her health, her good name, and threatened with the loss of her means of livelihood, at one fell swoop, cannot be expected to get on."

"Mr. Wells, I don't like the tone which you assume towards me."

"Mr. Allison, I shouldn't like it if you did."

For one moment Allison stared at the librarian, and Wells glared unflinchingly back. The magnate was mad in earnest now. "By God! Mr. Wells, you're the only man in this city who dares treat me with disrespect, and I won't have it!"

"By gad, Mr. Allison, it's because I'm probably the only one who thoroughly knows you. Wait till I tell all about your demands regarding Miss Wallen, and you'll find others in plenty."

"You can't, without looking elsewhere for a position."

"I can, for the position is looking for me, and the only reason I haven't accepted it is that I mean to stay right here until full justice has been done my stenographer,--full justice, sir. If that young lady were to place this case in the hands of even a tolerable lawyer, yours wouldn't have a leg to stand on."

"You don't mean she's going to law!"

"It's what my wife says would serve you right; and I agree with her. Just let this community know that solely on the statements of a cur you kicked out of your own employ you had defamed that brave, honest girl, and there'd be a tempest about your head compared to which this riot was a zephyr."

Allison's wrath was cooling now. He sank back in a chair and stared gloomily at the librarian. "Where is that" (gulp) "Elmendorf?" he finally asked.

"In jail, I hope; in the gutter, the last time I heard of him, being pommelled by her brother. Major Cranston and Mr. Forrest are looking for him."

"What do they want?" asked Allison, suspiciously.

"Several things; one is to find out how much he will admit having told you, and how much to hold you solely responsible for."

Allison fidgeted for a moment, and then turned again upon the librarian. "You mean to tell me that you think she's entirely good and honest and all that, do you?"

"No. I told you I knew she was."

"Well, then, what does it mean that Forrest is trying to hunt up or run down my witnesses?"

"It simply means that he's a gentleman who intends to defend the girl whose name you have coupled with his."

"Why don't he come to me? He hasn't been near my house since he came back," said Allison, in a tone of complaint. "He hasn't given me a chance to--fix things. Who was fool enough to tell him?"

"You, principally, by your reception of him. He knew all about it before he came here to me. Of course he hasn't been to your house, and probably never will go there again. I wouldn't in his place."

Allison pondered painfully awhile. "Well, I suppose this thing is beginning to get around the neighborhood?--people are talking about it?" he queried guardedly.

"Beginning?" was the answer. "Lord, no! It began the day you shouted the whole business so that everybody in the library could hear. Of course people are talking, but not as loud as you did."

"And you say she's down sick and can't see people. Of course if I've been--made a victim of in this matter by that fellow Elmendorf--why, damn him, he's been trying to make up to my own daughter! she had to order him out of the house,--of course I want to straighten things out. I withdraw my demand for her discharge, under the circumstances; and if I might send her a check--or something, in reason----"

"You might, if you wanted to see how quick it would come back."

"Why, hang it, Wells, what *should* a man do? What can a man do?"

"Sit down and write her that you have made a consummate ass of yourself. That might not be a delicate way out of it, but it would be telling the truth. Anyhow, you've got to do something, and that right soon. My wife tells me that her one idea is to get well enough to come over here for one day, just to confront her accusers. Then where'll you be, and your invaluable witnesses?"

Allison went home and had a conference with his sister which left that lady dissolved in tears. It was a brutally hot July afternoon, and he ordered the carriage for a drive in the Park and bade Florence drive with him, and obediently she went. There wasn't a whiff of breeze off the lake; it all came pouring from the hot prairies to the southwest, and everybody looked languid and depressed. The sun was almost down, and the walks and roadways in the Park were but sparsely occupied. Slowly the heavy family carriage rolled along the smooth macadam and drew up, with others of its kind, near a shaded kiosk where a band was playing. Presently from under her parasol Florence caught sight of a familiar figure. Leaning against the door of an open livery carriage, a tall man in straw hat and white duck suit was chatting with the occupants, one a middle-aged woman, with a gentle, motherly face, the other a slender girl in deep mourning, reclining languidly as though propped on cushions. Allison, anxiously watching his daughter, saw the light in her eyes, the faint color rising in her cheeks; and he, too, looked, then reddened, for all that other party seemed to face him at the instant. The tall man in duck came promptly around and stood beside them, bowing coldly to the father, but raising his hat and holding out his hand to Florence. She took it, her eyes not downcast, but seeking his.

"I am glad to see you out, Miss Allison," he said, in frank and cordial tone. "You were looking far from--yourself the night we met in front of the club. I hope you are well?"

"I am--better," she answered, rather faintly, "and I had hoped to see you--before this."

"That was why I went to the club that night," he answered, gravely. "How is Cary?"

"Oh, he's just miserable, because pa--father kept him cooped up and wouldn't let him out to the riots. He was simply mad when he heard of your experience with the mob. But you are coming to see us?" she finished, looking appealingly at her father.

"Yes, Forrest," said Allison, "I wish you would. There's a matter I want to talk to you about."

"Possibly the same that Mr. Elmendorf is to bring up at department head-quarters to-morrow afternoon, which I believe you will be invited to hear," said Forrest, calmly. Then, turning once more to Florence, he held forth his hand. "I am very glad to meet you again, Miss Allison," he said, "and to find you looking better. But now I must return to my friends." And, bowing again to her, but almost ignoring Allison, he walked away, and was soon in earnest talk with the ladies in the open carriage.

"Do you know who they are?" asked Florence presently of her father.

"Yes. One is Mrs. Wells, wife of our librarian. The other is a Miss Wallen, one of the library employees. She has been ill.--Go on, Parks," he said to his coachman, and they drove silently home.

"He came and talked with me," said Florence to her aunt that night. "He was polite and kind, and didn't seem angry,--didn't say anything, but--he went--he said he must go to his friends,--to his *friends*, do you understand? We're no longer--no longer of them." Then she turned and sought her own room.

And there was an invitation for Mr. Allison,--a very pressing invitation, for an aide-de-camp delivered it personally,--a request that Mr. Allison should be at head-quarters the next afternoon at four o'clock; and Allison went. He was received by Captain Morris, who expressed the general's regrets at being unable to see him in person, and was ushered into a room where were Colonel Kenyon, Major Cranston, and Lieutenant Forrest, still in service dress, and two of the senior staff-officers. These latter came forward and shook hands with the magnate, the others simply bowed.

"See if Mr. Elmendorf is anywhere about," said Captain Morris to a messenger. But it was ten minutes before that intellectual party appeared. The great strike had collapsed, the leaders were under the indictment of the law, and this particular agitator's occupation, like that of hundreds of his hapless dupes, was gone. Never-theless it pleased him to lurk about the neighborhood until fifteen minutes after the appointed time, so that he might be the last to arrive and might thereby keep the so-called upper classes waiting. The moment he arrived the chief of staff proceeded to business.

"You set four o'clock as the time you would appear to make your charges, Mr. Elmendorf, and we've been waiting here a quarter of an hour."

"Affairs of greater importance, sir, occupied my time."

"Oh, yes; our janitor tells us that you have been communing with yourself over a glass of beer in the saloon across the way for the last hour.--Gentlemen, I received a letter from Mr. Elmendorf yesterday morning, which I will read:

"'SIR,--Having been informed that Mr. Warren Starkey, a clerk in your em-ploy, has been discharged because of his having been accused of revealing to the press certain facts relative to the circumstances under which Lieutenant Forrest was twice ordered away from Chicago, this is to inform you that unless Mr. Starkey is immediately reinstated I shall consider it my duty, as an accredited correspondent of numerous newspapers of high repute, to publish all the facts in the case as well known to me, and to demand the dismissal of Lieutenant Forrest. That you may know I speak by the card, I purpose calling at your office at four P.M. to-morrow, at which time, if you see fit, the gentleman and those he may claim as his friends can hear the grounds on which I base my demand. Let the laws which oppress the poor and friendless now apply to the proud and powerful.

"'MAX ELMENDORF.'

"Now, Mr. Elmendorf, Mr. Starkey has been discharged, and has not been re-instated. We'll hear him first, and then you."

"Very good, sir. Though I seem to be alone in the lions' den, I shall not flinch from my duty even in the face of all this array that has been carefully selected from among mine enemies."

"They are exactly as indicated by yourself," coldly answered the colonel. "Send in Starkey."

And Starkey came,--Elmendorf's one weak victim among head-quarters force,--and Starkey was in a sorry plight. He told his story ruefully:

"I supposed this gentleman was all right. I used to see him with the officers. He was with them every day or two for hours. Then he made himself pleasant and sociable, and used to get me to lunch, or treat to drinks sometimes, and seemed to know everything that was going on. I didn't know anything whatever about Mr. Forrest's affairs except what he told me from time to time, and I believed what he told. Perhaps I did let on I knew more. He got me to drinking, and God only knows how it all came about. That reporter came to me and said that Mr. Elmendorf had told him this and that and Captain Morris had told him more, and then he got things up around the Lambert and around Forrest's lodgings, and asked me if 'twasn't so that Forrest had been ordered off on account of things happening there. Well, I suppose perhaps I did say that it was so, but I never dreamed that he'd make what he did of it. And then when the chief clerk caught me drunk and accused me of the whole thing I broke down and owned up to everything, and I've been a--well, I've just been that man's dupe."

The unhappy ex-clerk was withdrawn. Mr. Elmendorf cleared his throat in readiness to speak. Forrest, with a smouldering fire in his eyes and with compressed lips, sat gazing sternly at the ex-tutor. The others, with faces indicative of various shades of contempt and indifference or indignation, not unmingled with the curiosity which one feels in studying some uncommon type of animal or man, silently awaited his remarks. "I will begin by saying that my suspicions in this case were aroused long months ago," said Elmendorf, when the judge-advocate of the department suavely spoke:

"Kindly spare us your suspicions, Mr. Elmendorf. You promised facts, and, as time is short, owing to your own delay, we desire facts alone."

"The facts," said Elmendorf, nettled, "are that the gentleman in question, while posing as a man of honor and a welcome guest in a most estimable family circle, has long been secretly laying siege to the affections of a young and comparatively friendless girl, with such success that their relations became the talk of the neighborhood. I found that she had been seen at his lodgings after dark, that they were frequently seen alone together as late as midnight, and that they were often alone in the private rooms at the Lambert. These facts were so well known that when he was suddenly ordered to leave Chicago last winter the explanation arrived at by common consent was that the general sent him off to his regiment to avert further scandal, and that his second orders were for practically the same reason. It is notorious that because of this affair the girl has been threatened with discharge from the position she holds, and so I am here to say that since this poor clerk and this poor girl are made the sufferers and the only ones, I, as the ever ready representative of the people, demand the prompt punishment of the real offender, whom doubtless his class would shield. Nothing but my dislike of involving a poor working-girl in further scandal and trouble has held me silent until now."

"I see," said the judge-advocate, reflectively; "and you have intimated that in order to spare her further publicity you would be willing to abandon your purpose, provided----?"

"Provided Mr. Forrest tender his immediate and unconditional resignation from the service, and I be furnished written assurance that it will be accepted, also admission that my statement as to the cause of his sudden orders to leave Chicago was true."

The scene in the office that sultry afternoon was something to remember long days after. Cranston couldn't help thinking what a blessing it was that the breeze at last was blowing fresh from the lake and the white caps were bounding beyond the breakwater. It was a group worthy of a painter's brush,--Elmendorf's sublime confidence in the criminality of his fellow-man and the unassailable integrity of his own position, Kenyon's attitude of close and appreciative study of this unique specimen, Cranston's twitching lips and clinching fists, Allison's almost apoplectic face at one moment, contrasting oddly with the infinite consternation with which he contemplated his own probable connection with the plot the next:--the speaker was a monument of conceit and "cheek,"--might even be a lunatic, but what--what could be said of himself? The chief of staff was fuming. Forrest was inwardly raging, yet by a strong effort maintained, as he had agreed, utter silence, leaving to his friends their own method of conducting the affair. One officer alone seemed to be deriving entertainment from the situation: the judge-advocate had never had a professional treat to compare with it.

"Before committing ourselves to any promise, Mr. Elmendorf," said he, most blandly, "you will pardon me if I refer to what seems a trifle weak link in your chain of evidence. You say the young lady was in the habit of visiting Mr. Forrest's lodgings. How often have you seen her there?"

"I said she was seen there. I did not keep watch."

"On Mr. Forrest's *lodgings*, no. But how often was she seen there?"

"I am not prepared to state. Once is considered enough, I venture to say."

"How often did the witness tell *you* she was there, Mr. Allison?" asked the judge-advocate, turning, to his consternation, upon that gentleman.

Allison went crimson in an instant. "Well, I paid so little attention. It was all so frivolous," he stammered.

"Yet he was the witness named by Mr. Elmendorf, I believe,--the only one; and you had him come to your office and you questioned him there, did you not?"

"I did, yes, but the impression passed away almost immediately. The man wasn't worthy of confidence."

"When you hear his story you may think otherwise," said Elmendorf, with a contemptuous sneer.

"I have heard," said the judge-advocate; "but we'll hear it again.--Send Starkey's friend in here," he said to the messenger; and presently in came a hangdog, corner-loafer specimen of the shabby-genteel young man, supremely impudent on his native heath, but wofully ill at ease now. "This is your reputable witness, Mr. Elmendorf."

"I protest against indignity to my witnesses or browbeating of any kind. This is not a court, and he's not on oath."

"Certainly not. He's saved us all the trouble by telling the truth beforehand.--Now you can tell us how you came to chase the young lady into that door-way," said the judge-advocate, turning suddenly on the shrinking new-comer.

"Well, sir, I'd been drinking, and I thought she was--a girl I knew."

"Yes? and when you caught her in the vestibule what happened?"

"Nothin' much. She fought, and the door flew open, and----" here the shifting eyes wandered around until they rested on Forrest--"this gentleman kicked me out. I wouldn't 'a' said anything about it, only--him there found me afterwards." And he nodded at Elmendorf.

"Didn't you declare to me you'd seen the lady going in there with him? Didn't you see them together late at night up near her own home?" asked Elmendorf, excitedly.

"Well, you took me up and showed 'em to me."

"Didn't you tell me you knew she often went to his rooms?"

"Well, you asked me if I hadn't seen her, and I said no, and then you asked if I didn't think it was more'n likely, and----" Here Starkey's friend faltered.

"That will do," said the judge-advocate. "You both knew very well then, and you know now, that it is an apartment-house, in which several families dwell, some of them friends of the young lady in question. You can go, young man,--I merely introduced that party as a specimen of the evidence for the prosecution. Now, Mr. Elmendorf, let me give you a specimen of the evidence for the defence.--Colonel," said he to the chief of staff, "would you mind saying in the presence of these gentlemen whether the faintest inkling of any such charge as this of Mr. Elmendorf's against Mr. Forrest had ever reached you?"

"Not a whisper."

"Were Mr. Forrest's sudden orders in any way the result of any such rumor?"

"Not in the least. He was selected by the general to make certain confidential investigations regarding the encroachments of settlers, boomers, etc., on the Oklahoma tract. It was necessary that the object should not be heralded beforehand by the press, and so we had to keep it quiet."

"There, Mr. Elmendorf; admitting these as specimen bricks of the probable testimony, we decline to reinstate the clerk, or to attach the slightest importance to your allegations at the expense of Mr. Forrest, and I am constrained to say that your propensity for meddling has got you into a nasty mess. So far as head-quarters are concerned, we've done with you. Now I'll leave you to settle with the friends of the young lady." Here Elmendorf made for the door.

"I'm not to be assaulted, and----" he began; but Allison blocked the way.

"You lied to me and mine," he cried. "You declared on your honor that gentlemen high in authority in this office told you the reasons you gave for Mr. Forrest's summary orders to quit Chicago. I demand now to know whether it was not that poor devil whom you've ruined here,--Starkey. Answer me."

"What good would it do?" whined Elmendorf, shrugging his shoulders. "Would not my statement be promptly denied? ***Noblesse oblige***, sir; the first business of these Knights of the Sword is to stand together, and woe betide the knave who dare accuse one of them. But if you'll be guided by my advice, Mr. Allison, you'll look well to your own vine and fig-tree, lest the despoiler----"

But here Allison hurled himself upon the fellow and grasped him by the throat. "You whelp!" he cried, banging the luckless head against the door-post before any one could interfere. In an instant, however, the officers had seized him, shaking the tutor loose. Madly sped the latter to the elevator, but, finding Starkey and his crestfallen friend awaiting him there, he turned and dashed down the stairway, his ex-witnesses after him.

For a moment there was silence in the office, while Allison recovered breath. Bowing coldly to him, Colonel Kenyon, with Cranston and Forrest, turned to leave the room.

"Mr. Forrest," said the magnate, stepping hastily forward, "I am more rejoiced at your vindication than I can say. Of course I see I've been led into doing you an injustice, and I hope you'll permit me to make amends."

But Forrest declined the outstretched hand and thrust his own within the breast of his uniform.

"You have amends to make elsewhere, Mr. Allison," he answered, with lips that trembled despite his efforts at control, "and a wrong to right beside which mine is insignificant. Good-day, sir."

And so they left him.

CHAPTER XVII.

The regulars were gradually withdrawn from the Garden City, as old-timers loved to call Chicago, and Kenyon with his sturdy battalion was among the first to be restored to his own station. The crusty veteran left the home of his boyhood to resume duty at his proper post, and left with feelings somewhat mixed. "We never had more temper-trying work to do," said he, "and there isn't a man in the whole regiment that wouldn't rather stand six months Indian-fighting than six hours mobbing in Chicago. It's my own old home, so I've got a right to speak the truth about it. For years its newspapers, with one exception, have made it a point to sneer at, vilify, and hold up to public execration the officers of the regular army. During the past four or five years the lampooning and lying have been redoubled, and it is like heaping coals of fire on their heads that the very regiment they have abused the most was the most conspicuous in Chicago's defence. *We* had no picnic, but the Fifteenth simply had hell and repeat,--the meanest, most trying, most perilous duty, from first to last. Those fellows were scattered in little detachments all over Cook County, and faced fifty times their weight in toughs, and carried out their orders and stood all manner of foul abuse and never avenged it, when if any one of those young captains or lieutenants commanding detachments had lost his temper and let drive the lightning sleeping in those brown Springfields, there'd 'a' been a cleaning out of the rabble that would have thinned the ranks of one political party in our blessed country, at least. Oh, we're glad enough to get away and see the change of tone in the Chicago press; but it won't last."

And Kenyon's was by no means an exaggerated statement. In the far-spreading course of the great strike "the regulars" came in for many a hard knock from the mob and for not a few from the press. At one point experienced railway-hands, not mere ruffian rioters, wrecked the track at a trestle in front of a coming troop train, hurling the engine, with its gallant guard of half a dozen artillerymen, into the depths below, crushing or drowning them like rats. At another point, when baffled in their efforts to overturn a sleeping-car in front of a patrol engine, and dispersed by a dozen well-aimed shots, the rioters impanelled their coroner's jury, and declared the red-handed participants innocent spectators and the officer and his men murderers. At a third, when a great railway centre was found in the hands of the strikers and the troops were ordered to clear the platform, one surly specimen not only refused to budge, but lavished on the captain commanding the foulest epithets in a blackguard's vocabulary. The crowd outnumbered the troops by twenty to one. The faintest irresolution or hesitancy would have been fatal. One whack with the sword knocked the fight out of the bully, and, while he was led off to be plastered in hospital, the maddened rioters held their indignation meeting, and not only they, but high officials eager for their votes, united in denouncing the officer to the President of the United States, declaring the victim a model citizen, sober and peaceable, and the captain drunk, foul-mouthed, and abusive. The press of the neighborhood aided in spreading abroad the utterly false report of the affair, with the usual result of the temporary humiliation and distress of the officer and his friends, the inevitable official investigation, and the prompt verdict, "The officer deserves commendation, not condemnation." One paper, within five days of its original report, announced that it had discovered that it was the civilian who was drunk and who used the foul language attributed to the officer. It furthermore said that the officer had done just right; but this was the single and phenomenal instance. The other papers, like Elmendorf, probably reasoned that if the officer wasn't the blackguard they had striven to make him appear, he might as well have been.

These are specimens of experiences too well known to all concerned. "May the Lord preserve us from any more riot duty!" said Kenyon, piously, as they steamed away across the Illinois prairies; "but," he added, "I'll bet ten dollars to ten cents the politicians will get us into more and worse another year."

Yet even such scenes have their humorous side. It was Daniel O'Connell, I believe, who defeated the female champion of Billingsgate by calmly referring to her as the hypothenuse of a right-angled triangle, which was something utterly beyond her powers of repartee: it was he, at all events, who silenced another virago with the cutting response, "Sure every one knows, ma'am, ye're no better than a parallelogram, and you keep a whole parallelopipedon concealed in your closet at home;" and it was one of the trimmest, nattiest, most punctilious of our captains who stood in front of the silent ranks, listening in apparently absorbed attention to the furious tirade lavished on him by the spokeswoman of the mob, a street drab of uncommon stature and powers of expression and command of expletive. Winding up a three-minute speech with the remark, "I could pick ye up and ate ye, only the taste would turn me stomach, you white-livered, blue-bellied son of a scut," the lady had to pause for breath, and the soldier looked up from under his hat-brim and mildly remarked, "Madam, you're prejudiced," whereat even some of her sympathizers forgot their rancor and roared with laughter, and the idolatrous rank of his soldiery doubled up like so many blue pocket-rules, and the newspaper men chuckled with glee. By tacit consent, apparently, the Chicago papers were saying as little as possible against the regulars just then, and many a bright fellow who owned that he hadn't known anything about them before, except what he had read in his paper in the past, found many a friend among them and many a cause for writing of them in a new and different vein.

Cranston's old home was decorated in style the day the cavalry marched away. Mrs. Mac had the old guidons and a big flag swung out on the porch, Mac in his most immaculate uniform standing at the salute. Many an eye in the long, dusty column danced at sight of the honest couple, and one young fellow, their graceless nephew, now a recruit in Captain Davies's troop, braced up in saddle and fixed his eyes fiercely on his file-leader, and for fear of the stern avuncular injunction to "Kape yer eyes to the front, there!" couldn't be induced to peep at Aunt Mollie as she swung a tattered guidon that had been carried by Mac in the ranks of "C" troop many a year before. Captain Davies himself rode out of column and held forth a cordial hand to the old sergeant, as the last troop went clinking by. "We'll make a soldier of the boy, sergeant, as you tried to make of me when I joined," said he; "and if he has half the stuff there was in his uncle it'll be no trouble at all."

And so they went on up the avenue, with hats and handkerchiefs waving adieu and cordial voices shouting approving words. Presently, riding at ease now, they filed along under the beautiful facade of the Lambert Memorial, and, glancing up, Cranston saw at the broad bow window the familiar features of Mr. Wells and caught his joyous "Hurrah!" By his side, smiling and nodding and kerchief-waving, was his buxom helpmeet, one arm thrown about a fragile, pale-faced girl in black. Off came Cranston's broad campaign hat; he bent low over the pommel of his saddle, ay, and looked back again with admiration in his eyes and a fervent "Thank God!" upon his lips. There were decorations in plenty, and enthusiastic demonstrations, too, from a wide portico, "crowded with prominent society people," as the papers said, when a few moments later the column swung by Allison's impressive home; but here the major merely raised his hat and neither bent nor bowed.

Riot duty over for the time being, Mr. Forrest was recalled from the command of his company to a desk at head-quarters and bidden to complete the maps and reports of his Oklahoma work. The maps he went at methodically enough, but the report he hesitated over. "No," said Wells, in response to his call and question, "Miss Wallen is not ready to resume work at the Lambert, and it is my belief she never will be." Then he looked keenly at the officer's face, and was gratified to see the deep shade of anxiety and distress with which it was instantly covered. "She'll be **well** enough; it isn't that," he continued; "but the girl is proud and sensitive, as any lady has a right to be, and she hasn't forgiven Allison. Oh, yes, he sent her a sort of apology,--five lines of somebody else's fault and ten pounds of fruit. She gave the fruit to Mart's hopeful family, and I think she gave Allison the devil. I didn't see her letter, but the old man dropped in here the other day to ask when she'd be back, and incidentally remarked that she seemed to be rapidly recovering, if fifty pounds of temper to the square inch was any indication. 'How the mischief was I to know,' said he, 'that hundreds of girls had to work in offices at night, had to find their way home late at night, and that much of their work was dictated to them during the day and had to be typed before early morning?' Even if he didn't know, by gad," said Wells, bringing his fist down with resounding whack on his big desk, "it's time he did know that this country isn't France, and that these brave girls who are honorably earning their own bread, and often, as was the case with her, supporting whole families, are entitled to the respect, yes, by gad, the reverence, of every man with a grain of decency in him. This is America, by the Eternal!--the one country on the face of the globe where an honest girl may go wheresoever her work may call her."

"Amen to that!" said Forrest, "But do you mean that she will not return here?"

"Not unless she can be induced to withdraw her resignation. She comes to live under our roof to-morrow, you know. That good fellow Cranston has given Mart pay work. Her plan is to join forces with her old friend Miss Bonner and reopen her typewriter down town, and I find she has a will of her own."

This, too, was something Mr. Forrest became convinced of, even had he not suspected it before. Though still sorrowing deeply over her mother's death, Jenny was able to receive some callers by the time the troops were going, and very prettily she thanked her friend and customer, as she was pleased to call him, for the flowers sent so frequently during her illness. Despite the faint color with which she had welcomed him, Forrest could not but see how pale and fragile she looked, and the slender white hand that he had watched so often flying over the clicking keys seemed very limp and listless now. It only passively responded to the warmth of his clasp. In fact, it hardly could be said to respond at all. She was reclining in an easy-chair. A soft breeze, playing through the open window, rippled the shining little curls about her white temples, and Forrest drew his chair close to hers.

It was the first time they had been alone together since the night following his home-coming in the late spring, the night of the luckless dinner at Allison's, the night in which, leaving her to work alone at the Lambert over his rough notes, he had gone, as she believed, to spend the evening with his *fiancee*, the night when with almost frenzied fingers she worked to finish every word of his report that he might find it ready on his return, and that she might find, as she did, her way home without him. Then had come the sudden cloud of her mother's serious illness, of Mart's disappearance, the gloom of the strike, the crash of the riots, the blow of her mother's death, a grief the more pathetic because for several years mother and daughter seemed to have reversed their relative positions and the child had become the protector, guardian, and provider. Then the brutal wrong of Allison's accusation, told her with such well-simulated sympathy and reluctance, but with such exquisitely feminine stab in every sentence; the collapse, the struggle, the suffering, the half-reluctant convalescence--and the sudden sunshine of that afternoon when he turned from the carriage of the girl to whom he was declared engaged, let her drive away without another glance, and stood there, tall and stalwart and manly, his soft brown eyes fastened on her face,--hers, Jenny Wallen's, a penniless, motherless, homeless working-girl. Mrs. Wells had hugged herself with delight all the way back, and would have said no end of foolish things but for her patient's prohibition. Even the prohibition had not kept her afterwards from telling Jenny how Forrest had refused his hand to Mr. Allison, refused once more to set foot within his doors, and what, what could that mean?

But the girl, despite her woman's heart, had a clear brain and cool judgment. Holding herself in honesty, independence, and integrity the peer of any man she ever heard of, brave, proud, and self-reliant, she had schooled herself to study the difference between his social surroundings and her own. Wells had spoken of Forrest's proud and powerful kindred in the East, of a mother and sister who held their heads far higher than ever could John Allison, who forty years before was but a train-boy peddling peanuts for a livelihood. Even in the wildly improbable event of her soldier knight's learning to love her, what madness it would be to expect his people to welcome her, what madness to think of being his without that welcome! Even if through love for him they opened their arms to her, what would they say to Mart and his brood? Jenny's sense of the humorous prevailed over her troubles at this juncture and made her laugh at the contemplation of that mental picture. Then she bristled again with honest pride. Mart was her own brother, anyway, her father's son. He had been a dear boy and she very fond of him in the old days; he had married beneath him, weakling as he was; she'd stand by Mart and work for his wife and babies; they would learn to love Aunt Jenny, and she would forget she ever had cried for the moon or learned to love a soldier. She didn't love him! She wouldn't! But here were boxes of exquisite cut flowers that had been coming in for a fortnight, and here was the sender, his chair close to hers, and he bending still closer. Then he began to speak, and his voice--how utterly different it sounded now from that in which she heard him say good-by to Florence Allison! She wasn't strong yet. How could she control the throbbing of her heart?

And then the room seemed to begin a slow, solemn waltz, even when she closed her eyes and firmly shut her hands, for his first words were, "I have a world of things to say, and only this one blessed evening in which to speak. I am ordered to my regiment at once."

Coming home later that night, Mr. Wells found the partner of his joys and sorrows a tearful, lonely wreck on the parlor sofa. Jenny had disappeared. For all explanation Mrs. Wells drew him by the coat-sleeve into the room, shut the door behind him, precipitated herself upon her shoulder, and sobbed, "She--she--she's refused him."

"Well, I suppose she thought he belonged to Miss Allison."

"No, no. It isn't that at all: it's pride. It's obstinacy. I don't know what to call it. He told her--he told *me* there had never been such a thing as an engagement between Miss Allison and himself, and that there probably never would or could have been. I could see he was cut to the heart, that he loves our brave Jenny deeply, truly, and there isn't any quixotism about it. But she--why, the girl's just marble! It was he who called me and stood there with such sadness and reproach in his eyes and told me what he'd told her and begged that I should plead with her when he was gone, but she only covered her face, with the tears trickling down through her fingers, and when he had to go she stood up like a little queen and said she thanked him and honored him, and even assured him that there was no other man on earth she cared for, but no, *no*, NO, was her one answer to his plea that she would be his wife. She will not even let him write to her."

And Wells comforted his wife as best he could, but there was no comforting himself.

That was the first of August,--the hottest, dryest ever known along the lake, yet the dismal fog-horn tooted day after day and night after night when not so much as a single tear could have been wrung from the ambient air. It was all on account of the smoke-clouds that obscured the sun and shut out the horizon weeks at a time, for the whole Northwest was one blaze of forest fires, and Wells grew crabbed and ill tempered at his desk and snapped at his new typewriter until, between the smoke and the tears, her eyelids smarted. He delighted in bullying Allison when-ever he saw him. The magnate had offered Miss Wallen a permanent position and a good salary in his own office, and marvelled at her refusal. She still occupied her pretty room at the Wellses', but solely on her own conditions,--that she should pay her board. She reopened her typewriter in the big business block down town, and seemed to gain health, color, and elasticity in her daily tramps to and fro. Business seemed to prosper, now that the urgent need was over, and Jenny could have af-forded a better gown than that she chose to wear, but she didn't know how soon Mart might lose his job again, and, as he never saved for the wife and babies, she must needs save for them. Despite her prohibition, two letters came from Forrest. She read them, answered the first, gently and with womanly dignity in every line, but made no reply to the second. Frequently on her evening homeward walk she encountered Miss Allison riding or driving with some of the *jeunesse doree* of society. Hubbard was immensely attentive again, with many prospects, said his friends, of landing a winner, and as for Florence, it is due to her to say that she hid her woe most womanfully, if ever woe existed. Indeed, her Lady friends took much comfort in saying that she certainly had lost no flesh over her *affaire de coeur*,--in fact, quite the contrary. And twice did Jenny catch sight of Elmendorf, despite his promptitude in dodging around the corner. He had become a full-fledged journalist now, writing police reports for a daily and resounding leaders for a semi-occasional, but, like Cary, his former pupil, who was bent still on going to the Point, he had unlimited faith in the future.

So, too, have his fellow strike-leaders, and with some show of reason. Not that their principles have been endorsed, but that, just as in 1877, the active participants in the great riots have been allowed to go practically unpunished. The individual citizen who should heave a brick through the window of a crowded car, set fire to a sleeper, or slug a locomotive engineer at his post of duty would undoubtedly be sent to jail or the lunatic asylum, if detected; but when he conspires and combines with hundreds of others, thereby a thousandfold increasing the danger and damage, it becomes a delicate matter for office-holders to handle, and so, while the leaders are free to roam the land and preach sedition and rebellion, the criminal and vagabond classes, the ignorant and vicious, and the great array of foreign-born, foreign-bred laborers, eagerly await the next opportunity. The real sufferers are the native-born or naturalized citizens, who, listening to the false promises of professional agitators, have been egged on to riot and outlawry and have lost through them their situations, their savings, and, in some cases, even their little homes. This and what one of our ablest generals aptly described as the "affected sympathy" of the men in office, high or low, for the men in the workshop,--the more affected the louder,--brought about and will bring about again these scenes of tumult, riot, and rage that, but for the restraining hand of the regular army, would result in anarchy.

"We've had to step in between two fires many a time before," said old Kenyon, "and we'll have to do it many a time again. Any of you fellows who like that sort of thing may welcome this change of station, but I don't." And, indeed, marching orders had come. The autumn shaking up was distributing regiments anew, and once more Kenyon's battalions were striding through the Chicago streets,--Forrest, after sixteen years of subaltern life, wearing at last the new shoulder-straps of the captaincy. Cranston and his squadron, still retained within supporting distance of the old homestead, eagerly welcomed their comrades of the riot days, and no sooner were they fairly settled down in the fine quarters at Sheridan than the new captain was out of uniform and into civilian dress and speeding townward,--"to see Wells," he said. Forrest lived with Cranston a few days while getting his own quarters in readiness, and was there to help the major welcome home his wife on her return from Europe late in October. Going to town "to see Wells" seemed to prove a boot-less errand, for he came back with gloom in his dark brown eyes,--very pathetic gloom, Mrs. Cranston called it, and she, who had early gone to town to call on Mrs. Wells, began going rather more frequently than ever the major had contemplated, so interested was she in Mrs. Wells's boarder. "I want to know her well enough to be able to talk to her," she explained to her husband; but Cranston demurred. Possibly he knew from old experiences that one way not to influence a girl in favor of a friend was for Margaret to set to work to try. With the caution born of a quarter of a century of married bliss, however, he did not remind his better half of previous experiments. He meekly suggested that, as Forrest was likely to remain on duty all winter within besieging distance, it might be well to leave him and the lady to work out their own destiny.

"But it's so absurd, Wilbur!" said Margaret. "He is deeply, honestly, utterly in love with her, and she's worthy of every bit of it, if I'm any judge of a girl, and if she isn't careful she'll drive him away or anger him with her refusals to hear him. Why, she has refused even to see him, Mrs. Wells tells me, and--it's nothing but stubborn pride." Evidently, therefore, these two dames had been putting their heads together and were now in the combination to force Jenny to surrender.

Yet Jenny was right, knew she was right, and was to be moved neither by Forrest's pleadings nor by his friends' reproaches. There had been one long and painful interview between her and her lover soon after his return, and then very gently but very firmly she had told him that the matter must end then and there. She had asked him one question, and only one, in the course of that interview, and he could not answer her: "Mr. Forrest, what welcome would your mother, your sister, extend to me, a working-girl?"

Forrest said he really hadn't consulted them; he was seeking a wife for himself, not for the family. He said that once they knew her they would honor and love her as she deserved. But that wouldn't do. Miss Wallen had seen something of society leaders, and had formed her own opinion as to the law of caste. She had seen Robertson's charming play, too, and had her own views as to the matrimonial joys in store for its heroine. She had asked herself whether she would submit to being either tolerated or patronized by people who had wealth and position, to be sure, but not one whit more pride or principle, nor, for that matter, refinement, than she had. Down in the bottom of her brave heart was the craving of the woman to be loved for herself, to be appreciated for her true worth, but she believed that people in high position would not and could not accept one of her antecedents and connections, and she would have no concealment whatever. "Knowing me just as I am, just as I have been, knowing my brother and his people, you know well yours could not welcome me."

And Forrest knew even more. Divining one cause of Jeannette's refusal, he had told the whole story to his mother in the longest letter he had ever written,--and sorely he missed his typewriter in doing it,--and that letter proved a shock. The Forrests had built upon the story of his engagement to the beauty and heiress Miss Allison, and had long been awaiting his announcement to write the glowing letters of welcome, but here was a thunderbolt. Floyd had fallen in love with a working-girl, a shop-girl, a nobody, and actually wished his mother and sister to send gushing letters expressive of their approval and assurance of loving welcome. It was preposterous. They had expected a Florence and were told to be content with a Jenny. It was absurd in Floyd to point out that forty years ago Miss Allison's father was a peanut-peddler and Miss Wallen's a professor. Forty years in this country made vast changes. Floyd was simply pelting them with some of his ridiculous theories about the common people, their rights and wrongs. Lincoln, not Washington, was Floyd's ideal of the good and great and grand type of the American, and it had spoiled him. All this was what was said to one another in excited household chat. What was written was more diplomatic, but quite to the purpose. They could not endorse his choice, and he could not assure his proud, independent lady-love that they would. "He was awfully in love once before for years, and got over it," said Floyd's married sister, "and he'll get over this."

But there were those nearest to Captain Forrest about that time who arrived at a widely different conclusion. Jenny Wallen might have yielded could she have seen him and listened. Perhaps that was why she would not. It was no longer "Starkey's friend" who waylaid her on her homeward walks in the gloaming,--it was Captain Floyd Forrest, when he could get to town, and she took long, roundabout ways of reaching home and outmanoeuvred her soldier. With her whole heart crying out against her, pleading for him and home and love and protection, she stilled it like the sturdy little aristocrat she was, and would have none of him or his. "What can one do with a girl like that?" asked Mrs. Cranston of her grizzled major one bleak November evening on her return from town. "She has told Mrs. Wells that she is going to leave her roof and live with Miss Bonner away down on the south side, and it's all because Forrest is received at the Wellses' and she is determined not to see him." The major was hard-hearted enough to say he believed that interference even on Meg's part would only make matters worse.

But the captain heard of the proposed move, and then he placed in Mrs. Wells's hands a brief note. He was conquered now. Rather than see her leave the roof of such devoted friends, he pledged himself to vex her no more. Neither there nor on her homeward way would he seek to speak with her again. Jenny, yielding perhaps as much to the Wellses' pleading as to this, remained. What ever could be the out-come? was now the question.

CHAPTER XVIII.

Meantime the little blind god was working a combination of his own. One stinging wintry evening, when the wind was whistling from the northwest and a cold wave of most approved and vicious pattern had swooped down on Chicago, when the pavements were coated with ice and the populace with extra garments, and the visible features of pedestrians were unbecomingly red, a tall, soldierly-looking man, garbed in furs, was patrolling an up-town street and keeping anxious watch across the way. He had not promised not to look at her, at all events, and the thought of the fragile form he loved, shivering, possibly, in that bitter blast, had lured him from the Lambert to within sight of the Wellses' door-way. The yellow green of the wintry west was fading, the lamps were flickering in the gale, and the electric globes, swinging at the corner, threw black, shifting shadows across the pavement. The captain gazed wistfully up at a certain window across the way. She was not yet home, for all there was darkness. Then he peered along the sidewalk towards the avenue. A social function of some kind was going on, and a number of carriages were drawn up at the curb near a great stone house that faced the broader and more fashionable thoroughfare to the east, or else were moving slowly up and down, their coachmen thrashing vigorously with their arms to restore circulation in their numbed fingers. Forrest recognized the once familiar brougham of the Allisons', and conjectured that Florence, with her now desperately devoted Hubbard, was among the guests. At the eastward end of the street all was light and bustle, clattering hoofs and slamming carriage-doors. All to the west was gloom and silence; yet out of that darkness was he looking for the light, the one light, that could bring even momentary gladness to his eyes. He knew that on certain evenings it was her habit to stop and see how Mart's little brood was faring, and their new home was on a back street not four blocks distant. She was later than usual this evening; wondering why, he tramped westward towards the corner. He heard the swift hoofs of horses coming behind him, and the smooth roll of carriage-wheels. He saw sudden commotion and excitement among some children issuing from a baker's shop at the corner, and heard their shrill, eager voices, then the clang of gongs, the louder thunder of galloping hoofs, and the ponderous bounding bulk of a fire-engine as it came tearing down the cross street. Like a rushing volcano it dashed southward, leaving a trail of sparks and smoke, and then there was sudden warning cry. Some of the children, unmindful of anything except the engine, had sprung upon the crossing to see it go by, just as the carriage came spinning out from behind them. The coachman shouted, hauled at his reins, and did his best, but the little ones heard only the thunder in front, and in an instant, though almost sliding on their powerful haunches, John Allison's beautiful bays dashed through the frightened group, yet not before the alert soldier, with one spring, landed in their midst, brushing them aside, and then, with one shrieking little maid in his arms, went down on the icy pavement in the midst of a tangle of lashing hoofs and struggling, affrighted horses. How he got out he could not say. A giant policeman was tugging at his shoulder; ready-handed men were at the horses' heads, and, breathless, he stood erect, conscious of something wrong in one side, but mainly anxious about the child. She was picked up, stunned and senseless, and in the white glare of the electric lamp he recognized the features of Mart Wallen's four-year old Kitty. A sympathetic crowd had gathered. A young man poked a silk-hatted head from the carriage-window, and, with a face nearly the color of the Queen chrysanthemum in the lapel of his coat, besought Parks to hang on to his horses. A surly voice in the crowd said, "Damn your horses, and you too! If it hadn't been for this gentleman you'd have killed a dozen of these kids." Forrest's head was beginning to swim, but he took the limp little burden on his left shoulder. "Let me have her," he said. "I know where to take her. Bring a doctor to Mr. Wells's at once, please." And as he turned away he caught one glimpse of a fair, anxious face peering out across Mr. Hubbard's elegantly draped shoulder, and found that he could not raise his hand to his fur cap. "All right, Miss Allison," he smiled to her reassuringly. "Drive on." And then some one helped him in to Wells's parlor, and Mrs. Wells came fluttering down, all sympathy and welcome. Her deft, womanly hands stripped off the cheap hood and coat of the little sufferer; other friendly, sympathetic souls came in to help; and then, feeling oddly faint and queer, Forrest quietly stole away. Closing the glazed hall door behind him, he paused a moment in the vestibule, finding himself face to face with a slender form at sight of which even then his heart gave one great bound. Instinctively one arm was outstretched in longing, in greeting, and then at sight of him the form recoiled, and, cold as the biting wind that swept his cheek, he heard the brief sentence, "You have broken your word."

Bowing his head, conscious of rapidly increasing dizziness, raging at the thought of breaking down before her, yet smarting under the lash of her undeserved rebuke, he pushed blindly by and went forth into the night. The street was rocking like the steamer of the summer twice gone by as it pitched through the "roaring forties." He remembered trying to make his way back towards that corner--where the horses went down--there were friends there--and that big policeman--he'd help. The lamp-post leaned over and tapped him hard on top of the head. He tried to grapple it, but the right arm would not answer. Then his feet shot out from under him on the icy pavement, and the curb flew up and struck him a violent blow at the base of the skull.

Ten minutes later, as Jeannette Wallen was rejoicing over the returning consciousness of a sorely bumped but otherwise unharmed little maid, and hugging that precious niece to her heart, while the doctor administered a soothing draught, and Mrs. Wells was pulling off the pygmy shoes and stocking, the servant admitted an abashed citizen who faltered at the parlor door and mumbled, "Say, doctor, that gen'l'm'n that saved that little girl must 'a' got badly hurt. He's lyin' out here down the street--senseless----"

That was all Jeannette heard. Who caught little Kate was a question the distracted aunt never asked until many a long day after. Nobody caught *her* until, a dozen doors away, under the gas-light, in the midst of a little knot of neighbors, a battered, bleeding head was lifted from a rough coat-sleeve, and, folded in the slender, clasping arms of a kneeling girl, was pillowed on the pure heart where the baby curls were nestling but a moment before.

Fractured ribs and collar-bones yield not unreadily to treatment; even fractured skulls have been known to mend; and in a week, though dazed and bewildered, Captain Forrest was convalescing. Cranston and other fellows from the fort were in frequent attendance. The army surgeon from head-quarters had been unflagging, and Colonel Kenyon himself was at the railway station when the "Limited" arrived from New York, bringing a much-alarmed mother and sister, who relieved, if they did not entirely replace, certain other nurses at the patient's bedside. Upon their arrival, after three days and nights of vigil, Miss Wallen disappeared. She betook herself to Miss Bonner's refuge far down town, and just what Mrs. Forrest could have heard from the Cranstons, from her son's commanding officer, and from the fluent lips of Mrs. Wells, the reader may best conjecture, for it is a recorded fact that no sooner was her son out of all danger and well on the road to recovery than two ladies drove to the south side to seek this modest abode of working-girls and to call in person on Jeannette.

That afternoon came Cary Allison to visit his old friend the captain. Day after day had the boy been there to inquire, and it was good to see his rejoicing in the mending of the stalwart patient and refreshing to hear his comments on affairs domestic. Flo and her spoons just made him sick, he said, and the idea of having a Stoughton bottle like that for a brother-in-law was disgusting. "Why couldn't *he* have jumped out and lent a helping hand, instead of sneaking inside the coach and crying at Parks? Hubbard's a muff! I tell Flo he belongs to the family the squash was named for, and I call him Squash, too, and so does pa, though he's glad enough to rope him in to buying more stocks, I notice." It was plain that in Cary's eyes sister

Titania had found her Bottom and was enamoured of an ass. Brother-like, he had made her wince many and many a time, and now it was Forrest's turn.

"Say, cap, I do wish you'd come around and cheer the governor up a bit. He's been warped all out of shape since the strike, and seems to feel all broke up over home matters, too. He won't stay there at all. The last thing he did was to drive around to Wallen's and offer him a first-class clerkship, and now he's rowing with Wells because he won't let on what's become of your typewriter."

His typewriter? The girl he loved with all the strength of his being, honored and revered and longed to make his wife,--and the world could speak of her in that loose, pragmatical, possessive, chattel-like way. His typewriter! No more his than any man's who gave her employment. No longer his, in fact, since he was virtually forbidden her presence. He who had offered her his hand and name and love was actually of less account in the arrangement of her daily life than any one of the thousands who trod the pavement under her office windows, for they could offer work. Forrest threw himself back upon his pillow, buried his face in his arms, groaned aloud as the innocent youth went gayly forth into the wintry sunshine, and the doctor and the household of anxious women wondered what had happened to set back their impatient patient. Could it be, suggested that social prophet, his sister, that he was, after all, really interested in Florence Allison and chagrined at the news of her engagement, now formally announced? Might it not be, after all, that, as she had originally suggested, his apparent infatuation for Jeannette Wallen was mere sentiment, quixotism, proximity, and that he would speedily recover could they only get him away awhile? Surely it was worth the trial. His mother's health was suffering in the rigors of a Chicago winter. They had spent three months in St. Augustine each winter for years past, and but for Floyd should be there now.

It was arranged somehow. He was passive, submissive, indifferent. He knew nothing of the one wild moment of Jenny's break-down. He had never been allowed one hint of where his blessed head had been pillowed that bitter November night. The girl had pledged her friend to absolute secrecy. Removed on his convalescence from Wells's roof to his mother's rooms at The Virginia, Forrest saw no more of his hostess for several days. Then, with a three months' leave on surgeon's certificate, he was driven, under his mother's wing, to bid her adieu, and that night they were off for Florida.

"I'll never forgive him as long as I live," said Mrs. Wells. "He never gave me a chance to tell what--I can't tell you, Mrs. Cranston, but you **know**; and those two proud women have just got him between them now, and they'll never let him out of their leading-strings again."

"You don't know him," said Mrs. Cranston. "He'll break the strings and be back, or he isn't worth another thought of a girl like her."

But Jenny was not so certain. Never yet had she had opportunity to unsay the cutting words with which she had met him that bitter night. Time and again in her heart of hearts had she planned how those unsaying words should be said, and said just as soon as ever he came, but he came rather soon and suddenly.

They were great Christmas farers at Wellses'. With no children of their own, the sweet holiday season would have lost its sweetest charm but that Jenny was again with them. They rigged up a lovely Christmas-tree for Mart's babies, and summoned in sundry little waifs from the neighborhood, and had games and romps and laughter and merry voices. Later in the week there was a dinner at which the Cranstons and some fort friends appeared; there was a mistletoe bough that night and not a little coquetry and merriment, for Wells had invited the library girls and numerous young men to be present, and the customs of Old England were reproduced with characteristic American exaggeration. That mistletoe bough remained suspended from its chandelier, a reminder of the joys of the old year, even after '95 came knocking at the door, and in some odd way a little sprig thereof was found one evening to be clinging to the top of a cabinet photograph of Mr. Forrest which stood on the mantel shelf.

It was a sharp, cold January evening, and Jenny Wallen's soft cheek was glowing, and her eyes sparkling, as she tripped lightly up the stone steps, let herself into the warm hall-way, and peered into the parlor. No one was there. A bright coal fire blazed in the open grate. The pretty room looked cosy and inviting. The library beyond--"Wells's particular"--was dark. Mrs. Wells, said the maid, from the head of the kitchen stairs, had been home, but was gone over to the Lambert to meet Mr. Wells. So Jenny was alone. Some women lose courage at such times. She seemed to gain it. Drawing off her gloves and throwing aside the heavy cloak, she stood there in front of the blaze, her eyes fixed upon that unconscious portrait, her hands extended over the flames. What speaking eyes the girl had! What would be the words the soft, rosy lips were framing? With all her soul she was gazing straight into that unresponsive, soldierly, handsome face. With all her heart she was murmuring some inarticulate appeal, lavishing some womanly caresses upon the dumb and senseless picture. Then the little hands were upraised, and the next instant, frame and all, the shadow was nestled just where the substance had lain, clasped in those encircling arms, long weeks before. A moment or two it was held there, the sweet face bending over, the soft lips murmuring, crooning to it as a mother might to a precious child, and then it was raised still more, until those lips were pressed upon it long, long, long and fervently.

Then down went everything with a crash.

In striving to explain matters and set himself right in the eyes of his lady-love some hours later, Captain Forrest protested that he had had no intention whatever of spying upon, much less of startling her. They had speedily discovered at St. Augustine that it was useless trying to bring back this wayward son and brother, a man of thirty-five, to live without the heart so unmistakably in the keeping of the girl he'd left behind. "I have written to her--all you could ask, Floyd, my son," were at last the mother's words. "Go, and God bless you." And three days later he surprised Mrs. Wells. "I've just got to go out," said she, after a while, "and you've simply got to stay here. I'll leave directions that I'm out to everybody, and----" Then did that designing matron pick up his furs and deposit them--and him--in the library. "You're to stay here, mind, till I get back."

"But you didn't," interposed his hearer, reproachfully, at this juncture. "You burst in there like a--like a tiger, and scared me out of my seven senses."

"That was entirely your fault. I was merely trying to escape from the house. You see when I left Florida you were living, as I supposed, at Miss Bonner's, and as soon as you came in it was my cue to leave, in view of the ferocity of your remarks the last time we met here."

"Knowing how I must regret that, you need not have been so precipitate. It was what I think you gentlemen call a 'stand-off,'" said she, with a pretty grimace at the slang, "but--do you always take the roundabout way to reach the door?" Miss Wallen's lips were twitching with suppressed delight, and Captain Forrest was watching them with ill-suppressed emotion. He rallied promptly, however.

"Rarely, but in this case I flew--to pick up the picture you had dropped."

"Oh, the maid would have done that. She was promptly on hand."

"Yes, too promptly. So promptly as to inspire the belief that she suspected something was on foot when you--when I---- By the way, what became of that sprig of potato-vine, or chickweed, or something, that was on top of the frame? Mrs. Wells missed it as soon as she came in."

"It fell into the grate, I presume; but it wasn't chickweed. There's more of it if Mrs. Wells needs it," she added, nodding to the pendent spray beneath the chandelier. "It doesn't signify."

"Oh, I thought it did--at least I hoped so. Mistletoe generally does."

"Not when mistaken for potato-vine," she answered, yet her eyes were smiling at him.

"Jeannette," he said, impulsively, his deep voice trembling, as he stood close before her and strove to seize the little hand that was toying at her white, round throat, "mother's letter must surely be with you by morning. It is very hard to keep my faith and plead no more until she has pleaded for me. Must I wait? Will Miss Bonner bring it to you at once?"

"I--hardly think so."

"Then may I not go to-night, if need be, and get it? It was addressed, you know, to her care."

"Yes, so I observed."

"Jenny! Then you have it? You have read what she says? Oh, my darling! Then----"

And what imploring love was in those soft, brown eyes of his! What tenderness and longing and passion in the outstretched arms! She looked shyly up at him, trembling in spite of herself, but not yet yielding.

"You know I've had no time to more than glance at it," she said. "I had hoped to read it this evening, but, you see, visitors came in. I must read it all carefully to-morrow."

"Ah," he said, "you have me at your mercy. You wrung those promises from me, and now----" She backed away from him a bit, he looked so fiercely reproachful, but he followed. She upheld her hands in warning, and he strove to seize them, but they evaded him.

"You are proud, stern, unyielding," he said at last, and turned half helplessly away, then caught sight of the feathery spray now almost over her bonny, curly head. "If it were *only* Christmas time again! I'd claim the privilege of the mistletoe."

The room was very still a moment. She stood there with bounding, throbbing heart, her swimming eyes fixed on his strong, soldierly face, so powerful in its pleading, so helpless through his pledge. She saw that he would not break his promise, yet that her lightest word, her faintest signal, would unchain him. She saw even in the sterner lines about his forehead something of the look of utter weariness and defeat that hovered there the night they bore the senseless burden within those very doors, and in one great wave of tenderness, of answering love and joy and longing, the woman in her triumphed at last.

Only like a whisper, so soft, so tremulous was her voice, the needed words were spoken:

"Is it potent--only at Christmas?"

But he heard, and sprang to her and caught her in his arms. Little heroine though she was, what a tame surrender after all!

THE END.

The Codes Of Hammurabi And Moses
W. W. Davies

QTY

The discovery of the Hammurabi Code is one of the greatest achievements of archaeology, and is of paramount interest, not only to the student of the Bible, but also to all those interested in ancient history...

Religion   **ISBN:** *1-59462-338-4*   **Pages:132**
MSRP $12.95

The Theory of Moral Sentiments
Adam Smith

QTY

This work from 1749. contains original theories of conscience amd moral judgment and it is the foundation for systemof morals.

Philosophy ISBN: *1-59462-777-0*   **Pages:536**
MSRP $19.95

Jessica's First Prayer
Hesba Stretton

QTY

In a screened and secluded corner of one of the many railway-bridges which span the streets of London there could be seen a few years ago, from five o'clock every morning until half past eight, a tidily set-out coffee-stall, consisting of a trestle and board, upon which stood two large tin cans, with a small fire of charcoal burning under each so as to keep the coffee boiling during the early hours of the morning when the work-people were thronging into the city on their way to their daily toil...

Childrens   ISBN: *1-59462-373-2*   **Pages:84**
MSRP $9.95

My Life and Work
Henry Ford

QTY

Henry Ford revolutionized the world with his implementation of mass production for the Model T automobile. Gain valuable business insight into his life and work with his own auto-biography... "We have only started on our development of our country we have not as yet, with all our talk of wonderful progress, done more than scratch the surface. The progress has been wonderful enough but..."

Biographies/   **ISBN:** *1-59462-198-5*   **Pages:300**
MSRP $21.95

The Art of Cross-Examination
Francis Wellman

QTY

I presume it is the experience of every author, after his first book is published upon an important subject, to be almost overwhelmed with a wealth of ideas and illustrations which could readily have been included in his book, and which to his own mind, at least, seem to make a second edition inevitable. Such certainly was the case with me; and when the first edition had reached its sixth impression in five months, I rejoiced to learn that it seemed to my publishers that the book had met with a sufficiently favorable reception to justify a second and considerably enlarged edition. ..

Pages:412

Reference   **ISBN: *1-59462-647-2***   *MSRP $19.95*

On the Duty of Civil Disobedience
Henry David Thoreau

QTY

Thoreau wrote his famous essay, On the Duty of Civil Disobedience, as a protest against an unjust but popular war and the immoral but popular institution of slave-owning. He did more than write—he declined to pay his taxes, and was hauled off to gaol in consequence. Who can say how much this refusal of his hastened the end of the war and of slavery ?

Law   **ISBN: *1-59462-747-9***   **Pages:48**

MSRP $7.45

Dream Psychology Psychoanalysis for Beginners
Sigmund Freud

QTY

Sigmund Freud, born Sigismund Schlomo Freud (May 6, 1856 - September 23, 1939), was a Jewish-Austrian neurologist and psychiatrist who co-founded the psychoanalytic school of psychology. Freud is best known for his theories of the unconscious mind, especially involving the mechanism of repression; his redefinition of sexual desire as mobile and directed towards a wide variety of objects; and his therapeutic techniques, especially his understanding of transference in the therapeutic relationship and the presumed value of dreams as sources of insight into unconscious desires.

Pages:196

Psychology   **ISBN: *1-59462-905-6***   *MSRP $15.45*

The Miracle of Right Thought
Orison Swett Marden

QTY

Believe with all of your heart that you will do what you were made to do. When the mind has once formed the habit of holding cheerful, happy, prosperous pictures, it will not be easy to form the opposite habit. It does not matter how improbable or how far away this realization may see, or how dark the prospects may be, if we visualize them as best we can, as vividly as possible, hold tenaciously to them and vigorously struggle to attain them, they will gradually become actualized, realized in the life. But a desire, a longing without endeavor, a yearning abandoned or held indifferently will vanish without realization.

Pages:360

Self Help   **ISBN: *1-59462-644-8***   *MSRP $25.45* www.bookjungle.com *email: sales@bookjungle.com fax: 630-214-0564 mail: Book Jungle PO Box 2226 Champaign, IL 61825*

QTY

The Rosicrucian Cosmo-Conception Mystic Christianity *by Max Heindel*   ISBN: *1-59462-188-8*   **$38.95**
The Rosicrucian Cosmo-conception is not dogmatic, neither does it appeal to any other authority than the reason of the student. It is: not controversial, but is: sent forth in the, hope that it may help to clear...   *New Age/Religion Pages 646*

Abandonment To Divine Providence *by Jean-Pierre de Caussade*   ISBN: *1-59462-228-0*   **$25.95**
"The Rev. Jean Pierre de Caussade was one of the most remarkable spiritual writers of the Society of Jesus in France in the 18th Century. His death took place at Toulouse in 1751. His works have gone through many editions and have been republished...   *Inspirational/Religion Pages 400*

Mental Chemistry *by Charles Haanel*   ISBN: *1-59462-192-6*   **$23.95**
Mental Chemistry allows the change of material conditions by combining and appropriately utilizing the power of the mind. Much like applied chemistry creates something new and unique out of careful combinations of chemicals the mastery of mental chemistry...   *New Age Pages 354*

The Letters of Robert Browning and Elizabeth Barret Barrett 1845-1846 vol II   ISBN: *1-59462-193-4*   **$35.95**
by Robert Browning and Elizabeth Barrett   *Biographies Pages 596*

Gleanings In Genesis (volume I) *by Arthur W. Pink*   ISBN: *1-59462-130-6*   **$27.45**
Appropriately has Genesis been termed "the seed plot of the Bible" for in it we have, in germ form, almost all of the great doctrines which are afterwards fully developed in the books of Scripture which follow...   *Religion/Inspirational Pages 420*

The Master Key *by L. W. de Laurence*   ISBN: *1-59462-001-6*   **$30.95**
In no branch of human knowledge has there been a more lively increase of the spirit of research during the past few years than in the study of Psychology, Concentration and Mental Discipline. The requests for authentic lessons in Thought Control, Mental Discipline and...   *New Age/Business Pages 422*

The Lesser Key Of Solomon Goetia *by L. W. de Laurence*   ISBN: *1-59462-092-X*   **$9.95**
This translation of the first book of the "Lernegton" which is now for the first time made accessible to students of Talismanic Magic was done, after careful collation and edition, from numerous Ancient Manuscripts in Hebrew, Latin, and French...   *New Age/Occult Pages 92*

Rubaiyat Of Omar Khayyam *by Edward Fitzgerald*   ISBN:*1-59462-332-5*   **$13.95**
Edward Fitzgerald, whom the world has already learned, in spite of his own efforts to remain within the shadow of anonymity, to look upon as one of the rarest poets of the century, was born at Bredfield, in Suffolk, on the 31st of March, 1809. He was the third son of John Purcell...   *Music Pages 172*

Ancient Law *by Henry Maine*   ISBN: *1-59462-128-4*   **$29.95**
The chief object of the following pages is to indicate some of the earliest ideas of mankind, as they are reflected in Ancient Law, and to point out the relation of those ideas to modern thought.   *Religion/History Pages 452*

Far-Away Stories *by William J. Locke*   ISBN: *1-59462-129-2*   **$19.45**
"Good wine needs no bush, but a collection of mixed vintages does. And this book is just such a collection. Some of the stories I do not want to remain buried for ever in the museum files of dead magazine-numbers an author's not unpardonable vanity..."   *Fiction Pages 272*

Life of David Crockett *by David Crockett*   ISBN: *1-59462-250-7*   **$27.45**
"Colonel David Crockett was one of the most remarkable men of the times in which he lived. Born in humble life, but gifted with a strong will, an indomitable courage, and unremitting perseverance...   *Biographies/New Age Pages 424*

Lip-Reading *by Edward Nitchie*   ISBN: *1-59462-206-X*   **$25.95**
Edward B. Nitchie, founder of the New York School for the Hard of Hearing, now the Nitchie School of Lip-Reading, Inc, wrote "LIP-READING Principles and Practice". The development and perfecting of this meritorious work on lip-reading was an undertaking...   *How-to Pages 400*

A Handbook of Suggestive Therapeutics, Applied Hypnotism, Psychic Science   ISBN: *1-59462-214-0*   **$24.95**
by Henry Munro   *Health/New Age/Health/Self-help Pages 376*

A Doll's House: and Two Other Plays *by Henrik Ibsen*   ISBN: *1-59462-112-8*   **$19.95**
Henrik Ibsen created this classic when in revolutionary 1848 Rome. Introducing some striking concepts in playwriting for the realist genre, this play has been studied the world over.   *Fiction/Classics/Plays 308*

The Light of Asia *by sir Edwin Arnold*   ISBN: *1-59462-204-3*   **$13.95**
In this poetic masterpiece, Edwin Arnold describes the life and teachings of Buddha. The man who was to become known as Buddha to the world was born as Prince Gautama of India but he rejected the worldly riches and abandoned the reigns of power when...   *Religion/History/Biographies Pages 170*

The Complete Works of Guy de Maupassant *by Guy de Maupassant*   ISBN: *1-59462-157-8*   **$16.95**
"For days and days, nights and nights, I had dreamed of that first kiss which was to consecrate our engagement, and I knew not on what spot I should put my lips..."   *Fiction/Classics Pages 240*

The Art of Cross-Examination *by Francis L. Wellman*   ISBN: *1-59462-309-0*   **$26.95**
Written by a renowned trial lawyer, Wellman imparts his experience and uses case studies to explain how to use psychology to extract desired information through questioning.   *How-to/Science/Reference Pages 408*

Answered or Unanswered? *by Louisa Vaughan*   ISBN: *1-59462-248-5*   **$10.95**
Miracles of Faith in China   *Religion Pages 112*

The Edinburgh Lectures on Mental Science (1909) *by Thomas*   ISBN: *1-59462-008-3*   **$11.95**
This book contains the substance of a course of lectures recently given by the writer in the Queen Street Hall, Edinburgh. Its purpose is to indicate the Natural Principles governing the relation between Mental Action and Material Conditions...   *New Age/Psychology Pages 148*

Ayesha *by H. Rider Haggard*   ISBN: *1-59462-301-5*   **$24.95**
Verily and indeed it is the unexpected that happens! Probably if there was one person upon the earth from whom the Editor of this, and of a certain previous history, did not expect to hear again...   *Classics Pages 380*

Ayala's Angel *by Anthony Trollope*   ISBN: *1-59462-352-X*   **$29.95**
The two girls were both pretty, but Lucy who was twenty-one who supposed to be simple and comparatively unattractive, whereas Ayala was credited, as her Bombwhat romantic name might show, with poetic charm and a taste for romance. Ayala when her father died was nineteen...   *Fiction Pages 484*

The American Commonwealth *by James Bryce*   ISBN: *1-59462-286-8*   **$34.45**
An interpretation of American democratic political theory. It examines political mechanics and society from the perspective of Scotsman James Bryce   *Politics Pages 572*

Stories of the Pilgrims *by Margaret P. Pumphrey*   ISBN: *1-59462-116-0*   **$17.95**
This book explores pilgrims religious oppression in England as well as their escape to Holland and eventual crossing to America on the Mayflower, and their early days in New England...   *History Pages 268*

QTY

The Fasting Cure *by Sinclair Upton*   ISBN: *1-59462-222-1*   **$13.95**
In the Cosmopolitan Magazine for May, 1910, and in the Contemporary Review (London) for April, 1910, I published an article dealing with my experi-
ences in fasting. I have written a great many magazine articles, but never one which attracted so much attention...   *New Age/Self Help/Health Pages 164*

Hebrew Astrology *by Sepharial*   ISBN: *1-59462-308-2*   **$13.45**
In these days of advanced thinking it is a matter of common observation that we have left many of the old landmarks behind and that we are now pressing
forward to greater heights and to a wider horizon than that which represented the mind-content of our progenitors...   *Astrology Pages 144*

Thought Vibration or The Law of Attraction in the Thought World   ISBN: *1-59462-127-6*   **$12.95**
by William Walker Atkinson
                                                            Psychology/Religion Pages 144

Optimism *by Helen Keller*   ISBN: *1-59462-108-X*   **$15.95**
Helen Keller was blind, deaf, and mute since 19 months old, yet famously learned how to overcome these handicaps, communicate with the world, and
spread her lectures promoting optimism. An inspiring read for everyone...   *Biographies/Inspirational Pages 84*

Sara Crewe *by Frances Burnett*   ISBN: *1-59462-360-0*   **$9.45**
In the first place, Miss Minchin lived in London. Her home was a large, dull, tall one, in a large, dull square, where all the houses were alike, and all the
sparrows were alike, and where all the door-knockers made the same heavy sound...   *Childrens/Classic Pages 88*

The Autobiography of Benjamin Franklin *by Benjamin Franklin*   ISBN: *1-59462-135-7*   **$24.95**
The Autobiography of Benjamin Franklin has probably been more extensively read than any other American historical work, and no other book of its kind
has had such ups and downs of fortune. Franklin lived for many years in England, where he was agent...   *Biographies/History Pages 332*

Name	
Email	
Telephone	
Address	
City, State ZIP	

☐ **Credit Card**   ☐ **Check / Money Order**

Credit Card Number	
Expiration Date	
Signature	

Please Mail to: Book Jungle
PO Box 2226
Champaign, IL 61825
or Fax to: 630-214-0564

ORDERING INFORMATION

web: *www.bookjungle.com*
email: *sales@bookjungle.com*
fax: *630-214-0564*
mail: *Book Jungle PO Box 2226 Champaign, IL 61825*
or PayPal *to sales@bookjungle.com*

Please contact us for bulk discounts

DIRECT-ORDER TERMS

20% Discount if You Order
Two or More Books
Free Domestic Shipping!
Accepted: Master Card, Visa,
Discover, American Express

www.ingramcontent.com/pod-product-compliance
Lightning Source LLC
Chambersburg PA
CBHW080823020726
47501CB00009B/2398